OUTLAW

Troy Mason

outskirtspress

DENVER, COLORADO

Cover Art © 2013 Digital Media Imaging www.dmiwebsite.com. Author photograph © 2013 by Elizabeth Jeanne Photography. www.EJPhotography.org. All rights reserved - used with permission.

Outskirts Press, Inc.
http://www.outskirtspress.com

ISBN: 978-1-4787-1175-9

Outskirts Press and the "OP" logo are trademarks belonging to Outskirts Press, Inc.

PRINTED IN THE UNITED STATES OF AMERICA

This book is dedicated to:

Mom, who always encouraged me toward success…

Miss Lady, who believed in me every day and every step of the way…

BFF, who humbly finished second on virtually every ride we took.

Chapter 1

S ergeant Jason Broaduc had seen some screwed up situations in his nearly eleven months in Iraq. He had taken part of dozens of Civil Affairs missions that made no sense whatsoever. Building a school where no kids would ever be allowed to attend, building a hospital where no doctors or nurses even lived, but this one took the cake. Here in the Western region of the Al Anbar province, in a small desert town called Al Rubtah, he was providing security for his boss's mission to fire the police chief and the entire police force.

Not that the corrupt cops didn't deserve it, but it was only six months ago that the Americans hired a local Sheikh as the police chief in this known haven for terrorist activity. Within a month the Sheikh, who had presented himself as a friend to the American cause, hired several dozen family members and political allies with Anti-American sympathies as his staff of police officers.

That was when the real trouble started. As insurgent activity increased, Jason and his boss, Major Rick Campbell, had returned a number of times to instruct the chief on how to run a department and actually enforce the law. As was common in places like this, there was always an excuse for why no real action had been taken against the terrorists that increasingly called Al Rubtah home. First it was, "We don't have enough money for weapons and ammunition." Major Campbell provided over 200 brand-new AK-47s with magazines and 10,000 rounds of ammunition.

Next, "We do not have computers to keep proper records" Major Campbell provided a dozen laptops. Then it was, "We don't have a reliable power supply to keep the computers and the station running." Major Campbell provided a commercial diesel generator.

The straw that broke the camel's back came last month: "We don't have fuel for the generator."

Major Campbell had seen enough. He had provided over $250,000 of real estate, equipment, salaries, and facilities to calm the violence, yet terrorist activity had increased ten-fold. Recent intelligence revealed that insurgents from Al Rubtah had been the ringleaders behind a series of attacks and bombings against American forces 300 miles away in Fallujah. AK-47s recovered in these attacks were actually among the weapons that the Major had supplied to the chief for his department.

Jason stood in front of the stucco building that served as police Headquarters in downtown Al Rubtah. Major Campbell was inside firing the chief. These types of operations were impossible to keep secret in a country like Iraq, so not only the chief but also every officer on his force knew what was coming.

When Sergeant Broaduc pulled up, he was the second vehicle in a line of four Humvees. The plan was simple and straightforward: one Humvee parked diagonally on each corner of the building, facing outward so that every vehicle could see two others. Major Campbell and Gunnery Sergeant Robert Carbon would enter the building and meet the chief to conduct their business. Jason and the Marines in the other vehicles were to provide external security and ensure no one entered the Headquarters while the Major and the Gunny were inside.

Jason had a bad feeling about this mission from the start. There were many Iraqi police officers armed with American-supplied AK-47s and ammunition about to lose their jobs, their previous good standing with the Americans, their means of power and authority, and their only reasonable way to provide for their families. Most of these men were gathered on the street when the four Humvees reached their positions and came to a halt. The angry looks on the faces of the men bothered Jason, but not as much as the looks of grim resignation on a few of the others.

Anger can be met with force, and may dissolve and result in retreat. Resignation is, "I am going to die today." In that desperate mindset, where death seems the only option, Jason knew these few would do whatever they could to kill the Marines before they met their own fate.

Lance Corporal Christian Smith, a 19 year-old kid from Southaven, Mississippi, was manning the Squad Automatic Weapon, known as a "SAW," that was mounted in the gun turret atop Jason's Humvee. This light machine gun was an excellent anti-personnel weapon, and Lance Corporal Smith had proven his skill with it on a few occasions. Jason was glad the younger Marine was there.

Jason stood with his M-4 near the right front of the vehicle while the driver, Lance Corporal William Jeffers, stood at the left front. The sweat on the hot June day dripped into Jason's eyes as he surveyed the scene before him. Many of the officers milled about in front of the entrance to the Headquarters' courtyard. This placed them between Jason and the Humvee on the opposite front corner of the building. Staff Sergeant Rafael Aranda, a Texan and the son of Mexican immigrants, commanded that vehicle. He had been in the Marine Corps for nearly ten years, and this was his second tour of duty in Iraq.

Using his small intra-squad radio, Jason spoke softly. "Hey Staff Sergeant, I think we need to get these fuckers away from the front of the building. If shit goes down, we don't want them there when the Major and Gunny come out."

Staff Sergeant Aranda thought about it for a minute and replied, "Good call Sergeant. You work from your end and I'll work from mine. Get them all herded across the street."

With that, Jason and the Staff Sergeant began converging from opposite sides toward the soon-to-be-unemployed police. Before they were able to utter the first commands to move, an explosion from inside the building shook the ground and sent a massive plume of smoke and fire boiling skyward.

In that instant, the officers in front of the building turned their weapons on the Marines and opened fire at point-blank range. Jason turned back towards the safety of the armored Humvee, but was knocked flat on his face by a burst of AK-47 fire. His left leg was instantly numb and felt rubbery as he tried to regain his footing. Blood rushed into his face and he was flushed and nauseated. Ignoring these feelings, he struggled to his feet and yelled to Lance Corporal Smith to return fire with the SAW. As he reached the rear of the Humvee, bullets glanced and ricocheted all around, pockmarking the paint and creating spider-web designs in the bulletproof windows. Dust, smoke, rocks, and stucco peeled off the side of the Headquarters building as volley after volley of AK-47 rounds impacted on every side.

Only a few seconds had passed since the explosion, but Jason and the other Marines were returning fire into the intense crowd of police who were now fanning out across the street, firing as they went. Climbing up the back of the Humvee, Jason was shocked at the scene before him: Lance Corporal Smith was slumped in the gun turret, the SAW was silent. Blood was spattered across the roof behind Smith and a ghastly hole was in the back of his helmet.

The world turned red in Jason's eyes, and he was mentally removed from the moment. He could see himself from above, as if he were an observer of the scene and no longer a participant.

Clearly realizing that Christian was dead, but having no time mourn, Jason pulled his K-Bar knife and cut the strap that held his friend in the turret blocking the use of the weapon. As the young man's lifeless body fell into the Humvee with a sickening THUMP, Jason climbed into the turret behind him and pulled the trigger on the SAW. A smooth burst of rounds poured from the barrel, and Jason watched as an attacker fell to the ground in the street.

Regaining his sense of bearing and composure, but still observing himself from a million miles away, Jason skillfully maneuvered the SAW, killing an enemy with almost every burst from the barrel as AK-47 rounds bounced off the turret's armor. The intra-squad radios were alive now with the sounds of Staff Sergeant Aranda directing the fire from the machine gun atop his own turret and shouting instructions to the other two Humvees on rear corners of the building.

Intermixed with this was someone shouting "Corpsman!" the call for medical aid in the midst of battle. This was all surreal to Jason. More than a dozen enemy combatants lay dead in the street. The firing subsided for a moment, when Jason saw a car driven by a newly-unemployed police officer with a grim look of resolve emerge from behind a building near Staff Sergeant Aranda and his Humvee. In an instant, Jason realized this fanatic was a suicide bomber intent on blowing himself up alongside the Humvee.

Yelling, "Get down! Get down!" at the Staff Sergeant, but with no way to accurately fire the SAW and not endanger his fellow Marines, Jason lifted his M-4 and fired a single round through the windshield and into the vehicle bomber's head from 30 yards away. The man crumpled instantly, as the vehicle rolled to a stop and Staff Sergeant Aranda looked at Jason first with terror, then with thankfulness as he realized the gravity of what had nearly happened. Knowing that the car bomb could still detonate at any second, Jason yelled for Staff Sergeant Aranda to get away from the danger. As the Staff Sergeant ran behind the Humvee and its gunner ducked into the turret, the bomb detonated. Even from 10 feet away, the force lifted the 12,000-pound Humvee from the ground and flipped it over onto its roof.

The crater in the ground where the car bomb had stopped only moments before was now a smoking hole nearly six feet deep. The stunned Marines climbed out of the stricken Humvee as an eerie silence fell upon the street. Jason was aware of the sweat covering his body, but somehow he felt cold. Goosebumps appeared on his upper torso as he climbed from the gun turret and spoke into his radio. "I'm going inside to get the Major and the Gunny."

Staff Sergeant Aranda was dazed from the concussion of the explosion, but began to organize the remaining vehicles as Jason slid to the street from the roof of his Humvee. His left leg gave way as he landed, but he caught himself on the side of the truck. Sergeant Alfred Jamieson came up to accompany him into the Headquarters.

As soon as he saw Jason standing on the sidewalk, he shouted "Corpsman! Corpsman! Sergeant Broaduc is hit!" Jason looked down and saw that his entire left pants leg was soaked in blood.

"I'm okay," he shouted as he hobbled toward the entrance to the Headquarters building.

"You need a Doc!" replied the Sergeant.

Jason said, "The Doc can check me after we get the Major and the Gunny."

By now, the Staff Sergeant was calling for status reports from all his Marines over the radio. Broken reports came in of wounded Marines and crippled vehicles. Jason and Sergeant Jamieson entered the compound and found it still smoking and burning from the initial blast less than two minutes before. The stench in the air curled their noses and the ash burned their eyes as they shouted "Major Campbell! Gunny Carbon! Where are you? Yell out!"

Silence was the only response. Still, it did not take long to find the two Marines. The Gunny was lying under a doorway where the Arabic sign above read: Al Rubtah Chief of Police. This had been a gift to the chief from Major Campbell on the day they opened the new Headquarters.

The Gunny was unconscious and had blood covering the front of his body. Shrapnel holes in his pants were still smoking from the burning metal singeing the fabric when it entered his body. He was alive, but barely, and Sergeant Jamieson called for a Corpsman over the radio.

The Major was inside what was left of the office, clearly dead. As he had stood in front of the chief's desk, the concussion of the initial explosion and the shrapnel from its blast had killed him instantly. He landed across the office, lying on the floor, his back against the shattered wall as if he had decided to have a seat and rest for a while. He did not look restful though. Contorted into a shape no healthy human could ever achieve with blood stained as black as coal from the soot and ash blanketing the entire front of his body, he was still smoking from the fire.

Enraged at the scene, but undeterred in his role, Jason began dragging the Major out by his collar, struggling on his one good leg. The Corpsman arrived to attend to the Gunny while Sergeant Jamieson picked up the Major by the legs and helped Jason get him out of the building. Reaching Jason's Humvee, they lifted Major Campbell's body carefully into the back and laid him down as gently as they could.

Staff Sergeant Aranda called for a Medevac helicopter to evacuate the wounded and dead amidst piercing screams from an Iraqi woman crouched on a sidewalk across the street. In his earpiece Jason heard someone yell, "Somebody shut that fucking bitch up!" Looking up, Jason saw a young Private First Class Marine walking toward the woman. She was covered head to toe in Muslim garb, and she was hysterically moaning and shaking. A boy and a girl, neither more than four years old stood in shock on either side of her.

No more than thirty feet in front of Jason, the PFC reached her and screamed "Hey! Shut up! It was probably your fucking husband who did this! Now shut the fuck up!" As the woman looked up at the Marine before her, Jason could see the dead infant in her arms. Doubtless, she and her children were innocent bystanders to the ambush and ensuing firefight, and her baby had been killed in her arms in the crossfire.

She began frantically wailing again as Jason started half-limping, half-hopping across the street. The other Marines stood by the vehicles in stunned silence as the PFC drew his 9mm Beretta and held it to her head. "I said shut up bitch! Don't make me shut you up!"

These words had barely escaped the Marine's lips when Jason reached him and snatched the pistol away. Shoving the young PFC aside he yelled, "Get your ass back to the trucks! That's not how we do it shithead!" The PFC staggered back across the street with Jason following. Stealing one last glance over his shoulder, he could only see the pain in the woman's eyes. "I probably only prolonged the inevitable," he thought to himself.

As the remaining Humvees marshaled in front of the building to get everyone out, four Marines emerged from the Headquarters with the Gunny on a stretcher. The Corpsman was still applying bandages, and Jason got into his Humvee where Lance Corporal Smith's body was still laying in the back seat, the blood from his head wound pooling on the floorboards.

The stench of blood, smoke, sulfur, and burned flesh was overpowering in the heat of the western Iraqi afternoon. Jason, overwhelmed by everything, caved in to the nausea, and vomited on the street before he closed the door and ordered Lance Corporal Jeffers to drive. The small, damaged convoy sped through the streets to the outskirts of town just as two Medevac helicopters were landing.

The Gunny and a PFC who had been hit in the ribcage by a ricocheting AK-47 round were loaded onto the first helicopter. Jason was placed on the second chopper with the bodies of Major Campbell and Lance Corporal Smith. A Corpsman took off Jason's protective vest and assessed the wound from the rifle bullet. It had passed through Jason's left hip, and there were a few shards of pelvic bone in the exit hole. It was bleeding and was beginning to hurt as the chopper lifted off. Jason was no longer watching this scene from above. He was back inside himself again, where the pain, the fear, and the emotional tolls were all too real.

Chapter 2

Two weeks later, Sergeant Jason Broaduc was lying in a hospital bed outside of Washington, D.C. Surrounding him were other Marines, Navy Corpsmen, and soldiers recovering from their own wounds. Most of them were in much worse shape than Jason. His broken pelvis was already healing, and the doctors told him that they did not expect him to need another surgery to correct the bone, blood vessel, and nerve damage caused by the bullet that passed through his side.

His compatriots, however, had suffered and continued to suffer the most egregious pain. Many of them were amputees, and some were double amputees. One was blinded. Two others were burned so badly they would never live anything resembling a normal life again.

Jason knew he was lucky. The round through his side had passed under his protective vest, but five others had traced an upward path across his back, stopped only by the bulletproof plate in the vest. In any previous war that wound would have killed him, because bulletproof plates were a new item issued to Marines in Iraq. While he was still in the expeditionary hospital in Iraq, coming out of anesthesia from his first surgery, the Corpsman from the Medevac brought the damaged vest to him.

"You are one lucky motherfucker," he said.

"Not feeling so lucky, dude."

"Well, look at your fucking vest, man. See these holes in the back? That fucking Haji had your number. I've never seen a vest that stopped five fucking bullets! One, yeah. Two, rarely. But FIVE? No fucking way. I'm telling you. You're a lucky motherfucker."

"How's the Gunny?" asked Jason. He did not want to see the bloodstained, bullet-riddled vest anymore.

"He was on the other chopper. He's still in surgery, but he'll make it. He's pretty fucked up."

"And PFC Onver? He got hit too." Jason pressed.

"Yeah, he'll be okay too. He's out of surgery. Got pretty fucked up. Hit in his lung. It collapsed, but they sewed him back together. He's gonna make it."

"What's next?" asked Jason. "Where do we go from here?"

"You'll have to talk to the Doc about that. I don't know. I just wanted to give you your vest." The Corpsman set the vest on the floor by Jason's bed. As he turned to leave, Jason stopped him and said "Hey man. I'm still a little fucked up from all this shit. I wanted to say thanks for helping me on the chopper."

"Yeah, you were fading out from blood loss by the time we got in the air. We started an IV and gave you some blood and some shit for the pain. It knocked you out, but your blood pressure and heart rate were fine all the way here. You're gonna be fine. Got a ticket back to the States, I'm sure. We don't keep too many guys like you in country. Too much chance of infection. Say 'Hi' to the real world for me." The Corpsman walked out and left Jason in the stark confines of the recovery room to contemplate his future.

———)•((●))•(———

Now Jason was looking at a much brighter and infinitely more sanitary room. The ward in the stateside hospital had everything a person could want. TV, internet, board games, and a staff that managed to stay upbeat despite the pain that surrounded them every day. Jason was flipping through a motorcycle magazine when the door at the end of the ward opened, and several Marines in dress uniforms entered.

Jason had been around senior officers and enlisted Marines several times during his three years in the Corps, but this was the first time he had seen the Commandant and the Sergeant Major of the Marine Corps in person. A small staff of junior officers and a Gunnery Sergeant accompanied them. Jason was wondering what the occasion was for this visit, when the doctor who was with them pointed to Jason's bed and said, "Sergeant Broaduc is right over there."

Jason winced slightly from the pain in his hip as he began to sit up in the bed. The Commandant, a Four-Star General and the highest-ranking active duty Marine said, "Sergeant Broaduc, please don't get up. We're here to present you with some awards. I personally reviewed the after-action reports written about the battle in Al Rubtah, and the award recommendation from Staff Sergeant

Aranda. It's an honor for the Sergeant Major and me to be here, and we expect you to stay put and not get up."

"I'm confused, Sir," Jason said as he tried to sit up again. His mind was reeling as he tried to comprehend why the brass was in his ward.

One of the junior officers, a Captain who was a personal aide to the Commandant, stepped over and hit the button that raised Jason's bed to a sitting position. The hospital pajama top Jason wore was clean and white but he was nude from the waist down to prevent any unnecessary pressure on the wound. Jason held the sheets up to his stomach as the bed rose.

The Sergeant Major of the Marine Corps, the senior enlisted active duty Marine spoke next. "Devil Dog, we'll let you sit up, but stay in that bed. This is a special day for you; not too many Marines get an award like this, and I expect you to be comfortable when we pin it on you."

"Yes Sir," Jason replied.

"And don't call me Sir. You can save that for the officers. I used to be a Sergeant just like you. I fought in Desert Storm. Call me Sergeant Major."

"Yes Sergeant Major."

With that, the Gunnery Sergeant said, "Attention to Orders!"

Jason, still bewildered at what was happening, sat a little straighter, the nurses and doctors in the ward stood at attention, and all the other wounded men sat or lay still and silent as the Gunnery

Sergeant began to read from a scarlet and gold document folder he was holding.

"The Secretary of Defense presents the Purple Heart to Sergeant Jason Broaduc for wounds received in combat in the Al Anbar Province of IRAQ on June 25, 2004. Signed by the Honorable S. Hadley Brown, Secretary of Defense."

The Gunnery Sergeant handed the document folder to the Commandant who looked at it as the Sergeant Major pinned a Purple Heart Medal on Jason's pajama top. He shook Jason's hand and stood back as the Commandant handed the document to Jason, and shook his hand as well.

Both men returned to the position of attention as the Gunnery Sergeant read from a second document folder.

"The Secretary of Defense presents the Silver Star to Sergeant Jason Broaduc for gallantry in action against enemy forces in Al Anbar Province, IRAQ while assigned to Regimental Combat Team 4, 2nd Civil Affairs Group on June 25, 2004. During a routine civil affairs mission, enemy forces launched a preplanned and well-coordinated attack against Sergeant Broaduc and his fellow Marines. Though the machine gunner in his Humvee was instantly killed as the battle began, and though seriously wounded at the outset, Sergeant Broaduc ignored his own well-being and responded to the attack aggressively and decisively. He manned the machine gun and delivered accurate and deadly fire into the enemy, causing them to scatter and abort the remainder of their attack. As the enemy took cover in nearby buildings, Sergeant Broaduc saw a vehicle bomber approaching another Humvee. Shouting for his fellow Marines to take cover, Sergeant Broaduc fired on the assailant and killed him instantly. This action saved the lives of no less than three Marines, and brought the battle to its close. Still disregarding his own personal safety and the pain of his wounds, Sergeant Broaduc refused medical attention and entered the Police Headquarters to retrieve his Commander and Non-Commissioned Officer in Charge. Finding the Gunnery Sergeant gravely wounded, Sergeant Broaduc called for a Corpsman while he entered the office where his Commander had been killed. Only after all the other wounded and killed-in-action Marines received treatment did Sergeant Broaduc accept medical attention. Sergeant Broaduc's gallantry and courageousness under fire saved the lives of his fellow Marines and are in keeping with the highest standards of the Marine Corps and the United States Naval Service. Given under my hand, this 2nd day of August, in Year of Our Lord 2004. Signed, the Honorable S. Hadley Brown, Secretary of Defense."

The Gunnery Sergeant handed the award citation and a small blue box holding the medal to the Commandant. He looked briefly at the citation, opened the box and pinned the Silver Star on Jason's chest next to the Purple Heart. "Stand at ease!" he bellowed to the room. A collective exhale could be heard.

"Congratulations, Sergeant Broaduc. The Sergeant Major and I are both extremely proud of you. Thank you for your heroism."

"Thank you Sir," was all Jason could muster in response. The Silver Star? Really? He did not feel like a hero at all. The room was awash with movement as a photographer captured the moment for posterity, the Commandant and the Sergeant Major shook his hand and posed for pictures, while doctors, nurses, and other patients gathered around. Jason did not know what to think. He was happy when all the glad-handing ended and the entourage left. Jason took the first medal off his shirt. As he ran his thumb across the bust of

George Washington on the front of the Purple Heart he was reminded of the throbbing pain in his hip. He laid it down and took
the Silver Star off his chest to get a good look at it. Flipping it over
he read, For Gallantry in Action. Jason thought to himself, "I'm no
war hero. I was just doing my job." He tried to sleep in the quietness
of the early evening while the ward returned to its routine. As he
drifted off, he dreamed of AK-47 rounds bouncing off the gunner's
turret.

Chapter 3

The confines of the hospital ward continued to be home to Jason and the others. Occasionally one of the wounded warriors would get out and return to the real world, but sadly, there was always another wheeled in to take his place. Jason spent his recovery time looking through magazines of interest: Hot Bikes, Iron Horse, Sports Illustrated, and The Sporting News.

These always transported him back to the things he loved. From the time he was in elementary school in Paris, Tennessee, he played football, basketball, and baseball. A natural athlete, he excelled at every physical activity, but his focus was football. He participated in the other sports as a way to keep in top shape year-round so he would be ready for football season. He was a local star in junior high, and started at linebacker on the varsity squad during his freshman year in high school.

Jason's father worked at Parrish Auto Service. When Jason turned 16 and got his driver's license, his dad landed him a job working there as well. After school and every weekend, he changed oil and rotated tires while Mr. Parrish and Mr. Broaduc performed more complex repairs on the various cars. They allowed him the time he needed for football and school, but he managed to clock about 20 hours a week even during football season.

Jason's mother died from cancer when he was eight years old, and his father raised him single-handedly on a mechanic's salary. It was a modest existence, but they were happy in their small home near Puryear, Tennessee just north of the Paris city limits. Without a woman's influence in the house, it was a testosterone-fueled existence, with plenty of sports and war movies on the television. Jason and his father were close and often camped, hunted, and fished together. Jason's dad never missed a single game Jason played, even making the long drives to the other schools when the Patriots were away from home.

The Henry County High School Patriots advanced to the play-offs in both his Junior and Senior years, and a number of mid-level colleges recruited him. At 6'2" and weighing in at a chiseled 220 pounds, he could still run the 40 in 4.6 seconds and was utterly fearless on the field. Too small to be seriously considered by the bigger schools, he accepted a scholarship to Austin Peay State University in Clarksville, Tennessee.

In early December, just after the football season ended and Jason signed his scholarship, he approached his father as they were cleaning up the shop at the end of the workday. "Dad, I have enough credits to graduate this month, and I'm thinking about doing that instead of waiting until the spring."

His father looked up from the push-broom, leaving the greasy rags, metal shavings, and Oil-Dry on the floor unattended for the moment. "Why would you want to do that? If you're thinking you need more money, you know you can get some extra hours now that football season is over with. Besides that, taking a couple of college-prep courses this spring won't hurt you any. You know you're gonna need to buckle down on the books in college, scholarship or not."

"That's not really it, Dad. I'm looking toward what I need to do after college, and I'm not really sure what I want to be. Here's my plan: I'll graduate later this month, then I'll join the Marine Corps Reserves. They can send me to boot camp in the spring, and I'll still be back and ready to go in time for football season. Plus I'll be in better shape than ever. You know I've got to keep cracking on the physical stuff if I'm gonna compete in college."

"The Marine Corps? Are you serious? I don't know, son. Can't you wait until after college to decide that? That's a pretty big decision for you to be making at seventeen."

"Yes sir, I know," Jason replied. "But when I graduate college, my time in the reserves will be almost over, and if I don't like it, I can just get out. And if I do like it, I can become an officer. I just think this is a smart move for my future, whatever it might bring.

"Have you even considered the Army or the Navy?" Mr. Broaduc was trying to find an easier path for his son, not that he needed it … but really? The Marines?!

Come on, Dad, everybody knows the Marines are the best. Besides, you know that I would never be satisfied if I felt like I didn't take the biggest challenge."

"Jason, you know I support you no matter what you decide, but you need to think this over."

———— ◦《◦》◦ ————

With the impulsiveness of any seventeen-year-old young man,

Jason thought it over for nearly a whole day before he went to see the Marine Corps Recruiter on the courthouse square in downtown Paris, Tennessee. The Staff Sergeant who was working the desk that day was happy to see someone as fit as Jason walk through the door for a change, not just another teenager who thought being a Marine in real life was the same as the video games.

"What can I do for you, young man?" the recruiter asked as he stood and extended his hand for Jason to shake. He was shorter than Jason, but his dress blue uniform was the best among all the services, and he had a firm grip and a look in his dark eyes that said "Don't trifle with me."

"Sir, I would like to join the Marine Corps."

"Well, it looks like you've come to the right place. What I want to know is whether you have what it takes. Sure, you're big and strong. Probably play football over at the high school. But what matters to me is what's in here." He poked Jason in the chest right over his heart.

Jason did not flinch or look away from the Marine's deep stare. "Sir, I'm exactly who you want."

Although he remained rigid as ever inside his uniform, the recruiter smiled and seemed to relax. "Then have a seat and let's talk about what you can do for my Corps."

<hr />

Less than one month later, on a bitterly cold day in late January,

Jason found himself hugging his father goodbye and shaking his recruiter's hand as he left for boot camp. "Recruit Training" was the official Marine Corps term at Parris Island, South Carolina. When he stepped off the bus with forty-something other young men and stood on the yellow footprints outside the barracks in the middle of the night, he realized that as cold as the recruiter seemed at their first meeting, he had stumbled into a whole new world. The Drill Instructors had only one speed "FASTER", only one voice "LOUDER", and only one look "MEANER".

The next thirteen weeks were the most challenging Jason ever faced. When it was over however, he was no longer that cocky young kid who saw the recruiter back in December. He was an entirely new creation, a member of an elite fraternity, a United States Marine.

As the Honor Graduate for his Company, he was meritoriously promoted to Lance Corporal, and given a priority slot to attend the Military Police School at Fort Leonard Wood, Missouri. By the time he finished training, it was August, and he went to Austin Peay stronger and more mature than any other incoming freshman on the football team.

Chapter 4

These memories helped Jason to take his mind off the pain in his hip as he sat in his hospital bed. The doctors allowed him to walk around the ward with a cane, and he made several laps each day. He occasionally stopped by other hospital beds to speak with the occupants. That was how he met Ray Beach, an Infantry Marine from a poor family in Delaware. Jason was 23 years old; Ray was 19 and recovering from a fairly serious shrapnel wound to his left shoulder.

As the days passed, Ray and Jason began to spend more time talking and Ray would often come to Jason's bedside when Jason could no longer stand. They discussed their time in the Marine Corps, and Jason learned Ray was a PFC.

"Why haven't you been promoted?" he asked.

"Well, I was a Lance Corporal but then I had my girlfriend mail some Jack Daniel's to me in Afghanistan in a care package," Ray said, smiling. "Fucking Company Commander didn't like that, so he busted me. It was a good couple of drunks before that though." He laughed. "I was down to my last half-bottle before I got caught. I think they might have let me go, but the next day another package came in with three more bottles, and when they saw that they said,

'You're fucking toast, Devil Dog.'The rest is history."

"Dude that sucks, but I guess if you're gonna do the crime, you gotta do the time," Jason said, smiling back. "So, what are you gonna do when you get outta here and back into the real world?"

"Might give school a shot," Ray replied. "I got some other stuff that might make me some money if that don't work out."

"Like what?" asked Jason.

"Just things. You know. Gotta pay the bills somehow. I have friends in lots of places that might help me out, get me started, you know. I made some good contacts across the border in Pakistan, I could go do contract security for them. That pays like one-fifty a year tax-free. I'd be doing the same thing I'm doing now, only getting paid ten times as much."

"Sounds like that could work."

"How about you?" asked Ray. "What are you gonna do?"

"Well, I'm a Reservist but back in the real world, I'm in the Highway Patrol, so I'm going back there when they cut me loose. I may try to go back to school too, if I can work it in. I'm happy being a trooper, but you pretty much gotta get a degree if you're gonna go anywhere with it."

"OH! FIVE OH!" exclaimed Ray.

"Yeah, something like that," Jason laughed and immediately winced at the pain in his hip.

"I'm gonna go hit the rack," Ray said as he stood to leave. His left arm was in a sling. He was a little wobbly from the pain meds, and Jason watched him walk back to his end of the ward. He thought to himself, "That kid can either go good or bad, but he's going to be one or the other. There is no middle of the road for him." As this thought settled in Jason's mind, he realized, "There's no middle of the road for any of us. We're all extreme. We're all Marines. We've all been hurt. We're all going to be on one end of the spectrum or the other. Good or bad. That's all we're left with."

Chapter 5

In the early morning hours just after midnight, Jason woke up screaming and fighting in a cold sweat. The nightmare had returned him to Iraq and the ambush in Al Rubtah, only this time the screaming woman was his mother. He lay for several minutes trying to adjust his mind to the safety and setting of the hospital ward. The pain in his hip was excruciating and he briefly thought about calling to a nurse and requesting more medicine. These thoughts he dismissed almost immediately. He did not want to go back to sleep right now and the pain in his hip ensured he would stay awake as long as he wanted.

In the quiet of the ward, few others stirred. It was a common experience for someone to wake up screaming. All the patients were used to the interruptions and went back to sleep without letting it bother them. They were all on some combination of pain medication, anti-depressants, and other drugs that dulled the senses and made sleep possible. Before arriving at Walter Reed, they all slept in loud, dirty, and uncomfortable places. One trait they all shared as combat veterans, was an ability to sleep through just about anything.

The trail of events that led Jason into the Tennessee Highway Patrol began to unfold in his mind. During his first two years of college, he majored in Mechanical Engineering with a minor in

Business Administration. He continued to improve at football, making an impact on special teams in his first year by notching 12 tackles on kick-off and punt returns.

During his second year he saw more playing time, alternating with the senior middle linebacker, a starter for two years. During the last game of the season, just before halftime, the starter took a massive helmet-to-helmet shot from a pulling guard on the Murray State University squad. Unconscious for a few moments on the field, he was helped off on wobbly legs and Jason knew he would finish out the game for the Austin Peay Governors.

The second half of the game was a challenge as the Murray State line pounded on the defense, and continued pressing the attack despite being ahead by three scores. Jason and the defense took it personally, and the coaching staff continually yelled to them to pick up the pace and improve their play. Murray State was eight yards from the end zone with less than a minute to play. The coaches signaled to Jason the defensive play they wanted on third down. Jason leaned into the defensive huddle and made the call to the bruised and bloodied players. "Outer Zone, Delayed Mike Blitz," he said. This was a call for Jason to wait for two seconds after the play began then blitz up the middle. The hope was to confuse the offensive line into thinking the defense was in zone coverage and not account for Jason in their blocking scheme when he came up the middle.

The late fall afternoon sun was setting and the stadium lights were on as Jason and his teammates lined up for the play. The green turf on the stadium floor was in tatters from a season of big men doing battle on the field. The air was crisp and cool, but Jason felt none of the cold as he looked over the offensive formation. Only the most ardent Austin Peay fans remained in the stadium, and there was not much noise from the Murray State faithful situated near the opposite end zone one hundred yards away.

As the ball was snapped, Jason watched the quarterback drop three steps, indicating a quick pass. The two lines tangled in a mass of wills, growling behemoths fighting with all their might to attack or defend. Jason began his sprint to the left of the center who was helping his guard block the defensive tackle. As Jason approached the line, the guard spun off the block, and losing his balance, launched into Jason's legs. Jason's right cleat hung in a divot in the turf as the 330-pound lineman crashed into the side of Jason's leg.

The snapping of Jason's femur was the loudest sound on the field, and Jason could not remember being in more pain at any time in his life. The world was a blur of red hot flashes of light and Jason simultaneously wanted to run from the pain but every move he made laying on the turf only intensified the agony. The Austin Peay training staff ran onto the field even before the referee called the injury timeout. There was little they could do to thwart the torturous agony he felt. He lay as still as he could as they gently lifted him onto the stretcher and carted him off the field.

Two surgeries and two weeks later, he lay with his leg in traction at Vanderbilt Hospital in Nashville when his coach walked into the room with the Austin Peay Athletic Director. "The doc says that's the worst break he's ever seen", said the coach. He was a graying middle-aged former collegiate athlete who had never held a real job. The AD looked distracted, as if he had better places to be.

"Doc also says I'll be up and around in a couple of weeks," Jason said as he thought about the exams and other papers he would have to make up before he could even begin the spring semester. "I'll be on crutches, and I may not be ready for contact in the spring, but I'll sure be ready by next season."

The AD spoke next. With a detached look in his demeanor but trying to convey sympathy, he said, "There won't be a next season, Jason. The injury you suffered was just too severe. I'm afraid you won't be able to play football for Austin Peay anymore."

Jason felt his heart sink at the prospect of losing his sense of belonging – his place on the team. He looked to his coach. "Why?" he asked. "I'll be able to play. I guarantee it!"

"No Jason," said the coach. "We can't take the chance on you getting re-injured. The risk is just too great. With an injury like this, a re-occurrence could mean permanent damage, perhaps even loss of the leg. You've played your last down. I'm sorry."

Jason could feel his blood pressure rising. His heart pounded in his chest, his fists clenched the stark white hospital sheets in cold sweat. The pain in his leg intensified as he asked, "What do I have to do to prove that I can still play?"

The AD stared at him. As calm as if he were delivering a homework assignment, he said, "Jason, we cannot let you play anymore. This is an institutional decision based on your safety and the best interests of the university. As is the case in all athletic scholarships, there is a performance clause. Since you cannot play anymore, we are rescinding the scholarship at the end of this academic year. The scholarship allows us to terminate it immediately, but I have personally spoken with the university president, and he is allowing you to stay in school until the end of the spring semester. After that, you are free to reenroll as a non-scholarship student, but in either case, you cannot play football. Look at this as the opportunity to pursue a new direction, but the university cannot afford to keep a scholarship athlete in school who cannot play. The university will, of course, continue to cover your medical expenses related to this injury until the end of the academic year as well."

"Fuck you!" shouted Jason. "I gave you my blood, sweat, and tears, and this is how you repay me? Fuck you and the school!"

"Jason! Calm down!" the coach shouted back, slowly patting the air with his hand, but it was too late. Jason lunged sideways in the bed making a grab for the coach with his right hand. His fingertips just brushed the fabric of the coach's cardigan sweater, and as Jason fell from the bed the traction machine caught his leg and suspended him by the broken appendage. He screamed in a loud, guttural tone.

Both the coach and the AD were backing quickly away toward the doorway yelling for a nurse or a doctor. As the nurse entered, she called for others to help her lift Jason, now barely conscious from the pain, back into the bed.

Chapter 6

Jason began rehabbing his hip more seriously. He had his fill of the hospital ward. The psychologist visited him a couple of times, asking questions about his experiences, the nightmares, and flashbacks. Jason was honest in his answers, but like all Marines he was simply too tough to admit to any problems. Eventually the overworked psychologist told Jason he would be fine and then quit visiting. With so many critical cases of Post Traumatic Stress Disorder, he simply did not have the time to treat what he viewed as normal recovery from combat wounds.

Jason's hip continued to heal and he found himself daydreaming more often about the Harley waiting for him at the dealership in Nashville. Less than one month before being wounded, Jason had been tasked for the umpteenth time to accompany a load of captured AK-47s to Camp Liberty in Kuwait. He always enjoyed these trips. Camp Liberty had all the amenities of a modern stateside base. Fast food restaurants, good shopping, and even a credit union branch were all available at the largest United States base in Kuwait.

On this trip, Jason once again used his satellite telephone to call his friend Muhammed Ali Banji, a Kuwaiti national who held the contract to melt the AK-47s in a large furnace. "Muhammed, it's Jason. We're back on the camp, when can you come by and pick up the rifles?"

"Jason, hello. I can be there in two hours. In sha Allah." Jason knew this translated to "In God's time," and was Islam-speak for "I'll be there when I get there." Time and punctuality were things that simply never took root in the Middle Eastern world. Two hours could just as easily mean two days, two weeks, or never. Jason was not bothered; he knew Muhammed would be there before the day was out, because he did not get paid until he took the weapons, and one thing that had taken root was the universal love of money.

Jason locked the weapons in a CONEX shelter, and went to the Base Exchange. He had a personal mission on this trip as well. Making a beeline for the Harley Davidson representative, Jason introduced himself. He had met this guy before, but since the visits were sporadic and Jason never bought anything, the dealer did not remember him.

Actually, dealer was too strong a term. On many overseas bases, Harley Davidson had sales representatives who could offer genuine discounts to service members wanting to buy a new motorcycle and have it waiting for them at the dealer of their choice back in the states. They offered any number of customization options, and could have the bike delivered within a couple of months of the order.

"How's it going?" asked Jason as he approached the desk that served as the representative's office in the hallway of the Base Exchange.

The man looked up, smiled and said, "It's hotter than the gates of hell, but the AC in here is keeping me sane." He laughed at his own joke. He was middle-aged, frumpy, with lots of gray hair. He wore slacks and a long-sleeved shirt with the Harley Davidson logo imprinted on its left breast. His hand was extended toward Jason, who shook it and sat down in one of the two metal folding chairs across from the desk. "I'm Bill Parsons. What can I do for you today?"

"I'm Jason Broaduc, and I'm here to buy a bike." Jason smiled, knowing he had just made the man's day.

"Great! Just one?" he asked, laughing at his own joke again.

Jason smiled politely. "Yeah. Just one. Can't ride but one at a time."

"Okay. What'll it be?" He looked Jason in the eye as his own spirits genuinely lifted, knowing he would get paid this month.

"I want a Road Glide. Gloss Black. Sissy bar, luggage rack, and highway pegs."

"Those are nice bikes" replied the salesman, reaching for some paperwork. "Do you want exhaust, air filter, fuel injection remapping too?"

"No, I'll take care of that myself."

"Okay" replied the salesman. With the paperwork in front of him now, his pen poised over the form, he asked "Can I get your full name?"

Jason talked the man through all the paperwork, where to deliver the bike, when he would be back in the states, and the price. After they settled, Jason shook his hand, walked two doors down to the credit union and got a cashier's check for the full amount. The bike was his; he just needed to get home and pick it up.

After signing all the paperwork and getting a double Whopper with cheese from the Burger King, Jason's satellite phone rang. It was Muhammed. He was here and ready to get the weapons.

Muhammed hugged Jason in the traditional greeting when they met. They had spent a lot of time together over the past ten months. Jason had delivered literally thousands of weapons to Muhammed for destruction. AK-47s, pistols and other rifles of all shapes and sizes, shotguns, and even some Russian-made heavy machine guns were all turned over, destined for the melting chamber. The contract for destroying the weapons, like hundreds of other necessary war-time services, was given to the local populous to keep the United States in good standing with the government. Nothing is more wel-coming in a foreign land than several hundred million dollars being poured into the local community. Jason knew the Kuwaiti govern-ment kept most of the money and paid men like Muhammed only a fraction for the job they did, but no one complained because the money was still good and the work was easy.

"How's your family?" asked Jason as he released the embrace.

"Praise be to Allah, they are well. My cousin has started a spice exporting business. He buys them from suppliers all over the Middle East and sells them to wholesalers in America. He is making a for-tune! All glory to Allah who is gracious and merciful."

Jason found the constant references to Allah to be both annoy-ing and essentially meaningless, but members of that faith often felt that a failure to mention him would send them straight to Muslim hell. He tolerated it as part of a culture he really did not care to understand. He liked Muhammed, and he was one of the very few non-Americans Jason trusted in this land.

Muhammed and Jason counted the weapons together and

checked them off against the inventory list Jason brought from Iraq. They loaded them into Muhammed's 20-year-old jalopy that was formerly a functioning dump truck, and he disappeared toward the other end of the camp where a furnace would turn the perfectly good weapons into ash and a shapeless hunk of steel.

Chapter 7

As the dog days of August in the Washington, D.C. area gave way to some cooler nights in September, Jason's wound continued healing, and he was able to walk with no assistance. Sitting in the recreation area, he felt restless. Staff Sergeant Paul Tharpe, a very squared-away African-American Marine came in and sat across the table from Jason. The Staff Sergeant was the Administrative Chief for all the Marines at Walter Reed Hospital, and had only one clerk to assist him with the huge volumes of paperwork associated with dozens of wounded Marines constantly coming and going from the hospital.

"Sergeant Broaduc, the docs say you'll be released from the hospital before the week is out. I should have talked to you a long time ago, but we've been swamped here, plus you were still recovering and it seemed there was just never an opportunity. Anyway, your contract in the Reserves is set to expire at the end of the month, only two weeks away. If you are interested in re-enlisting, we need to get started on the paperwork ASAP. Whether you re-enlist or not, you're still leaving here in a few days, and we need to get you processed one way or the other."

Jason met the Staff Sergeant's stare and briefly considered his options. "I've thought about this a lot, Staff Sergeant. I think it's time I got on with my life. The Corps is great and it's been good to me, but this last couple of years have obviously been rough. I think I'm ready for a little normalcy."

"Well Sergeant," replied the Staff Sergeant as he looked at the Silver Star recipient before him, "nobody is going to argue with you. You have a great future in the Corps if you decide to come back, but you've done your part. Here's what we're going to do. I'll get the paperwork together, and when you leave here, we'll send you to your Headquarters in Nashville. They can finalize everything, and you will be free. It's been a real pleasure," he stood and extended his hand to Jason. "Fair winds and following seas, Marine."

Taking the Staff Sergeant's hand, Jason stood and shook it. "Thanks Staff Sergeant."

"I'll be back up here with the paperwork in a couple of days," he called over his shoulder as he walked to the ward's exit.

⸻ ((◍)) ⸻

Processing out of the Marine Corps was an easy and painless evolution for Jason. Just as Staff Sergeant Tharpe promised, he delivered the papers to Jason the day before the doctors discharged him. Within 48 hours, Jason was standing outside his company Headquarters in Nashville with an Honorable Discharge in his hand. The time to go back to the real world had come.

He went straight to the Harley dealership to pick up his bike. It was clean and perfect, just the way it looked in all his dreams since the day he handed the money to the Harley representative at the Base Exchange in Kuwait. The salesman in Nashville was in his late twenties, and he was serious about mastering his trade. "Mr. Broaduc, you really should consider our extended warranty plan. It could save you a lot of money down the road."

"No thanks," Jason replied as he looked over the chrome and the paint. He could not wait to hear the motor come to life and get pointed down the road to his house 120 miles to the west. "I can work on my own bike. If it breaks, I'll fix it."

"Are you sure?" replied the salesman as he feigned a concerned look. "It's a really good deal, and we can even give you a discount on your regular service. Pretty much everybody gets the warranty."

Jason spoke firmly, quickly losing patience. "I said 'NO.' Did you hear me the first time?"

"Yes I did Mr. Broaduc. Did you know the warranty even covers your tires? No matter how they get damaged, we replace them free. Even if you run over a nail. Are you sure you don't want to consider it?"

Blood rushing to Jason's head gave a pink tint to his vision. There was no real reason to be upset with this guy who was only trying to do his job, but Jason's patience was at its end. Grabbing the small salesman by the collar, Jason jerked him up to eye level. With his mouth only inches from the terrified man, Jason spoke in a low but intense voice that left no doubt about his intentions. "Motherfucker, I told you 'no.' Ask me again and it will be the last question that comes out of your mouth before I rip your windpipe out. Now give me my fucking keys so I can go." Jason released his grip with a slight shove that put the salesman off balance.

Terror was clearly written on the man's face. He backed away, keeping his eyes on his assailant as he moved toward the office to retrieve the keys. Others in the shop had witnessed the exchange, and a couple of other salesmen moved toward Jason but stopped when he released the man. The tension in the air subsided only slightly, and everyone went about pretending to continue what they were doing. No one was letting Jason out of their peripheral vision.

The manager came out of his office with the keys. The salesman apparently thought it was best to remain behind. "I'm sorry if there was some misunderstanding Mr. Broaduc. Please enjoy your bike and if there is anything else we can do for you, please give us a call." The demeanor of the manager left no doubt that he hoped Jason would never call or come back through the Nashville area again.

Taking the keys, Jason started the motor and let it idle for a moment while he put on his helmet. It was a beautiful day, and he was looking forward to the ride home. By the time he pulled away from the dealership, everyone inside was feeling genuine relief and mentally readying their version of the story to share with everyone they knew.

Chapter 8

The next day Jason saddled up his new bike and rode into the neighboring county to visit his Tennessee Highway Patrol Division Headquarters. He was not ready to go back to work but the Patrol is a brotherhood, just like a football team and the Corps, and the last place he still belonged. Jason wanted to let them know he was back so they could prepare for his return to the streets. As he pulled into the parking lot a trooper - the Sergeant who trained Jason when he was fresh from the academy three years before - was leaving the building with papers in his hand headed to his car. He watched as Jason approached on the motorcycle, not recognizing him after more than a year. The Sergeant was an African-American man who, at 6'6", stood considerably taller than Jason. He was the picture of fitness. His shoulders were broad, his waist was narrow, and the muscles in his arms looked like cords of steel. He wore his uniform with pride. His shoes had a mirror-like shine, as did his gun belt. The Smokey Bear hat on his head was pulled down low over his eyes. Jason had seen this man strike fear into the hearts of an entire 15-passenger van filled with college kids who had partied a little too much. Nobody messed with Sergeant Thaddeus Johns of the Tennessee Highway Patrol.

Parking the bike near the Sergeant's car, Jason turned off the engine. As he removed his helmet, the stern and serious expression on Thaddeus' face quickly faded into surprise, and then a big, toothy smile. He approached Jason quickly and gave him a firm handshake. "Welcome home, Trooper!" he exclaimed. "Damn it's good to see you again."

"Good to be back, TJ." Jason used the Sergeant's nickname. Nobody called him Thaddeus. He hated that name.

"When are you coming back to work?"

"I don't know," replied Jason. "I guess that's what I'm here to find out. Is Captain Barnes in his office?"

TJ's expression became suddenly serious. "Man, I guess you haven't heard. Barnes got transferred to Memphis. He's a Regional Commander now. We got a new Captain. Stan Tucker. I don't want to color your opinion, but this motherfucker is a Class-A prick. He just got promoted. He spent the last five years on the Governor's Protection Detail, and he thinks his shit don't stink. Never mind that he's been working in plain clothes and hasn't written a ticket or worked an accident since the 90's. Good luck when you meet him. I avoid that ass-wipe at all costs."

"Fuck man. Doesn't sound like it's gonna be a lot of fun, huh?" Jason said.

"I don't know, man. Maybe he'll like you. He needs to like some-body." TJ was smiling again. "It's good to see you. Let's get together for a cookout soon. Yvonne and I will have you out to the house for some barbeque and beer. You can tell me all about your war-hero shit." TJ shook Jason's hand once more and walked to his car. He was every bit the badass Jason remembered.

Jason knocked on the new Captain's door and was greeted with a gruff, "Who is it?"

"Sir, it's Trooper Broaduc. I'm back in the area and I wanted to talk to you about coming back to work."

A lengthy pause, then "Come in."

Jason entered the office and immediately noticed photos of the Captain wearing suits and posing with countless dignitaries. As part of the Governor's protection staff, he traveled with the Governor just as the Secret Service does with the President. In this role, he met high-level politicians from all over the globe, and judging by the tiny amount of empty wall space in the office, he never missed a chance to take a picture with them.

Standing in front of the desk, Jason was silent while the 35-year old Captain continued typing on his computer. He had not invited Jason to sit, and he did not seem like he was in a hurry to address the young trooper until he was good and ready. Jason stood there sizing up the Captain. He was a stocky man with a bit of middle-age belly roll beginning to form around his mid-section. He wore his hair in a tight crew-cut, and his clean-shaven face showed a strong jaw and high cheekbones. Jason did not doubt this guy could have been a good trooper if he could escape the fact that he was an arrogant ass who only cared about himself and his upward mobility. Apparently, he thought his time on the protection detail elevated him to some sort of celebrity status with the highway patrol, and thus he was above all the run-of-the-mill troopers like Jason and TJ.

After several uncomfortable minutes of ignoring Jason to prove the point that he was in charge, the Captain looked up. "Trooper Broaduc, I'm Captain Tucker. I transferred in here after you left to go play soldier." Jason could feel his blood boiling, but stifled the urge to explain the facts of life to the Captain. He continued, "I have to tell you, I have dedicated my life to the Tennessee Highway Patrol, and I expect every trooper who works for me to do the same. I don't have patience for confused loyalties. You left and this division has been short-handed ever since. You were only supposed to be gone a year; it's been 16 months. I know you were wounded," he waved his hand dismissively at Jason's hip, "but if you are going to work for me, we have to understand each other. I take this job very seriously, and I don't like having troopers here that I can't count on. Now what's your status with the Army?"

The world was turning red for Jason, the words "For Gallantry in Action" flashed through his mind, but he bit his tongue and reminded himself that this guy was his boss. At least for now, he was going to have to tough it out. It would end eventually. He began, "Well Captain, first of all I was not in the Army - I was in the Marine Corps. I was discharged last week, so you don't have to worry about me getting called away again. I'm here and that's that. I think we understand each other well. I'd like to talk about when I can get back on the job. I'm thinking November should work well if that's okay with you."

Looking absent-mindedly towards some papers on his desk, the Captain said, "Sure. What's another month without a trooper who hasn't been here in damn near a year and a half?"

Jason could feel himself losing control, but took a deep breath to calm himself. He pursed his lips and stood silently, not wanting to give the Captain any more ammunition.

"Here's what we're gonna do", continued the Captain in a tone that dripped with self-righteousness. "You will report here for duty at midnight on November first. All the troopers in this division got new cars while you were gone, but since you weren't here you missed out. There's a 1999 Ford Explorer sitting out back. Nobody's used it, but I'll have it ready to go before you get back. It's not pretty. In fact, it's a total piece of junk, but then again you should be glad you have anything at all. You can pick it up a day or two in advance." He picked up a sheet of paper from a stack on his desk. "It says here that you live in Henry County. Is that right?"

"Yes. I got my father's house when he died. It's off Highway 641."

The Captain gave Jason a look that he hoped would make Jason believe he knew exactly where Highway 641 was in Henry County, but Jason could clearly see his new boss had no idea. "Well, the bad news is that Henry County is full right now. As you know, there are five counties in this division. I need you in Dickson County. You're the junior trooper in the division, so until somebody moves or dies, you're just stuck."

The assignment to Dickson County meant a 75-mile one-way commute for Jason, and both he and the Captain knew it. In one colossal butt-fucking, Jason had just been given a vehicle that was probably the worst one still owned by the Tennessee Highway Patrol, and he had been assigned an area to work that would add nearly four hours of daily commute time in his new piece-of-shit state truck. He wanted to get out of there and clear his head. He needed a beer and some miles on his new Harley.

Jason arrived back at his own driveway just as the sun was setting. A large wooden box was sitting in front of his garage. After parking the bike, he saw that it had the return address of a facility in Iraq. Prying the lid off, he found his footlocker and all his other personal gear that was left behind when he was flown out of the country four months earlier.

The scent wafting up from inside the box was the staleness of the dirt and dust of Iraq. The smells instantly transported Jason back to the desert. The memories were flooding back, and he closed his eyes for a second to quell the upswell of anger and frustration that Iraq represented. Sitting next to the footlocker on the bottom of the box was his flak vest with the bullet-stitched ballistic plate still inside. There were bloodstains on the vest from his own wound as well as from the wounded he tended to during his final battle. The sights, sounds, and smells of that battle filled his mind. In an instant, he was vomiting in his driveway right next to the crate.

"Get a hold of yourself man," he thought as he heaved again. "You have got to be in control of this thing or it will kill you." He shoved the box in the garage and locked the door. Except for the Harley ride to and from the Highway Patrol Headquarters, this day had totally sucked. Thunderstorm clouds were gathering in the west. "Good," he thought, "the rain will wash away the vomit."

He opened a cold beer and sat in the darkness of his living room slowly sipping it while the rain pounded away at the town. Two hours later, he was still in the same position, with the same beer, thinking the same thoughts. He needed to cleanse himself of Iraq and he thought he knew just how to do it.

Chapter 9

The next day dawned, and Jason got an early start on unpacking the shipment from yesterday. His mind was clearer now, and he went about his task with grim determination. Opening his footlocker, he pulled out the socks, tee shirts, and boxer shorts, throwing them all into a 55-gallon steel barrel that served as the trash can for his garage. Underneath the clothing, he found a small green notebook that he used throughout his tour. In it were notes from mission briefs, but it also contained the contact information for everyone in his unit. Phone numbers, stateside addresses, and other information he might need.

There was still a month before he had to return to work, and he was going to spend it on his bike in a soul-cleansing ride. He needed to purge the ghosts of Iraq, and he was going to start by visiting the parents of Christian Smith, the 19-year old kid killed during that final battle.

Packing his saddlebags with the bare necessities of clothing, he straddled his motorcycle and backed it out of his garage. His bedroll was strapped to his luggage rack. The engine came to life, and he let the bike warm up while he locked the garage door and said goodbye to his house for a couple of weeks.

The weather was cool, but his leather jacket and chaps kept him warm as he sped down the backcountry roads pointing in the general direction of Memphis. Jason made it a point to avoid major highways and interstates when he rode. He enjoyed the sights, sounds and smells of the countryside, and he appreciated the slower pace he found away from the larger metropolitan areas.

He stopped for lunch in Covington, eating at a Mom and Pop diner that likely had been owned by the same family for 40 years. The food was good and he enjoyed listening to the old men talk about the weather, fishing, and local politics. It seemed the mayor might have damaged his re-election chances by spearheading a property tax increase to pay for upgrades to the sewer system.

Saddling up on his bike again, he left the courthouse square heading south down Highway 51. He gunned the engine at the city limits and roared toward Memphis. Christian was from Southaven, Mississippi, a suburb on the south side of town. He could be there before suppertime, and he wanted to meet Christian's parents before he looked for a place to stay for the night.

Highway 51 wound its way through some of the poorest neighborhoods in Memphis. The Road Glide was low on gas, and Jason stopped at a station with iron bars and bulletproof glass on the windows. The clerk, a young black girl with long weaves in her hair and a ring through her left nostril was running the cash register inside a small enclosure surrounded by more bulletproof glass. A small tray was underneath the glass so the customers could slide their money through. Jason noticed her fingernails were about three inches long and painted bright pink with small diamonds in the shape of roses on each one.

Sliding a $20 bill through the cash slot, Jason said, "I'm filling up with Premium on pump #2."

The clerk did not bother to look up or even speak as she took the money. She absentmindedly blew a bubble with her gum and sucked it back in with a loud pop. Jason walked back out and lifted the pump handle, setting the nozzle into his fuel tank and adjusting it to pump slowly, avoiding any splashes on the paint job. As the pump was running, he saw two black teenagers approaching. Their pants were sagging almost to the bottom of their boxer shorts and both wore oversized sports jerseys and ball caps with flat brims sitting crooked on their heads.

The pump automatically shut off at the $20 mark as the two boys approached Jason from the front of the bike. "Excuse me, Sir," the older of the two said. He was probably about 17 years old and had diamond earrings in each ear and four gold teeth in the front of his mouth. "Do you know what time it is?" he asked.

"No," Jason replied, holding out his hand to show that he was not wearing a watch.

"We need some cab fare to get downtown," the younger one said. He was no more than 15, but he was nearly six feet tall and well-muscled. "Can you loan us a dollar or two?"

This was sizing up to be an ugly situation. Each teen was standing just out of arm's reach on either side of the bike. Jason could not get to one without being vulnerable to the other. He turned his back to the pump and faced them, as his world began turning red saying, "Guys, I don't have any money for you, and it would be best if you moved on. I'm not the guy you want to fuck with."

"Yo motherfucker, what's yo problem?" said the older one. "You got sumpin against us? You don't even know us."

"Exactly," replied Jason, pulling his badge out of his jacket pocket. "And you don't know me, so keep on moving." He motioned down the street.

"Oh, you five-oh," said the younger one, taking a step toward Jason. "You think that scares us? We own this fucking street. You on our turf, and you under our law now."

The 15-year-old's mistake was getting too close. Jason grabbed his collar with his left hand and jerked him forward as he brought a straight right-hand punch into the youth's nose, breaking it and buckling his knees. Jason let him go as he fell straight to the ground between the gas pump and the bike. The other's hand flashed from under his shirt and came up with a knife. "You just signed your death warrant, motherfucker!"

"I doubt that," Jason said as he pulled his .45 automatic and pointed it at the kid. Fear filled the teenager's eyes as he took a step back. "Move on," Jason said and motioned down the street with the pistol. The young thug took off running and Jason returned the pistol to his waistband. The other punk was clambering backwards as he wiped blood from his face. He sat back against the gas pump and spit a stream of blood on the pavement. Jason looked back at the clerk. She was watching from the safety of her bulletproof enclosure and did not seem as if what she witnessed was too far from ordinary. Jason brought the motor to life and rolled out into the street, ready to put this urban nightmare behind him.

Christian's parents lived in a quiet home in a modest subdivision in Southaven. As Jason pulled into their driveway, he could see lights on inside. A banner with a gold star hung in a front window. His stomach was in knots as he approached the door. Before he could knock, it opened and Christian's father stood before him. He was not yet 50 years old, and was dressed neatly in khaki trousers and a button-down shirt. "Sir, I'm Jason Broaduc. I served with your son in Iraq."

Sadness flashed across the man's face. "Please come in," he said, opening the storm door and offering his hand for Jason to shake. "I'm Horace Smith, Christian's father." He called into the kitchen, "Emily, come to the living room. We have company."

As they passed through the foyer, Christian's mother entered the living room. She was an attractive woman in her early forties, and wore Capri pants and a flowered blouse. Her blonde hair was pulled up in a bun. Horace made the introductions and motioned for Jason to sit on the love seat while he and his wife took the couch. The wall above the couch held a large shadowbox containing an American flag, along with the Purple Heart medal and photo of Christian in his dress blue uniform. A final memorial to a son taken too young.

Jason continued, "As I was telling your husband, Mrs. Smith, I served with Christian in Iraq. He was in my squad. I wanted you to know that he was a fine young Marine and that he always did his job well. I was proud to have known him, and I'm very sorry for your loss."

Tears welled up in Emily's eyes. It was clear that the wounds were still fresh and the pain was still deep. "Thank you. Christian mentioned you several times. He always spoke well of you." Her voice cracked as she continued. "Were you with him on that day?"

Her husband took her hand in his and said, "The Marine Corps has told us very little about that day. Just that it was a combat operation in Al Rubtah. We have not heard from anyone else in the unit. Not even a letter from the Commanding Officer. Doesn't he traditionally write to the immediate family?"

"Well Sir, I don't know about that tradition and if it's followed today. What I can tell you is that our CO was also killed that day. It was a terrible fight. It only lasted a few minutes. I was also wounded along with our Gunny and some others as well."

Emily and her husband were both fighting back tears now. "Listen," said Horace, "we really don't need all the details. I don't think it will help at all, but we do have one question. Did he suffer?"

"Sir, there is no way he ever knew what happened. It was so fast, and he was killed by one of the first shots fired. I can promise you he never suffered at all."

"Thank you." Emily spoke through her tears. "I miss him." Her voice failed and her tears flowed in streams down her cheeks. Horace held her and gave Jason a look that showed his own pain and loss.

After several long and painful moments, they stood and dried their eyes. Emily gave Jason a hug. "Thank you so much for coming," she said.

Jason wanted to feel some closure on Iraq as he pulled away

from the Smiths' driveway. He felt he was on the path to healing, but it was not coming nearly as quickly as he hoped. The visit with Christian's parents was not the cleansing experience he expected. Instead, he felt conflicted and angry at the senseless loss, the parents' suffering, and the endless torment he experienced in night after sleepless night.

He rolled out onto the highway, heading west into the setting sun. He was looking for a hotel for the night, but did not really feel like stopping. The cool air was refreshing, and as long as he was on the bike he did not have to confront the loneliness night would bring. Crossing the Mississippi River into Arkansas, he quickly exited onto Highway 79 as darkness fell.

The temperatures dropped into the upper 40's and the wind was picking up as he pulled into a roadside motel in Hughes. The office was closed, but a sign indicated a number to call to summon the owner from his home adjacent to the building. Jason dialed it, and in short order he was dropping the duffle bag that served as his suitcase on the floor next to the double bed. He was tired from a long day of riding in cool temperatures and he really wanted a beer, but he knew he needed to try to sleep. There was no way he was going to try to hunt down a six pack in this sleepy town that clearly rolled the sidewalks up when sun dipped below the horizon.

As he lay on the bed in the darkness, he thought about Christian and Major Campbell. He knew he was lucky to be alive himself, but the pain of living with the memories, anger, and depression sometimes felt like more of a punishment than death. Hours passed and he slept fitfully, awake before the dawn.

Leaving the key on the nightstand, he pulled away from the motel as the sun rose behind him in the east. The final destination on this trip was before him: the town of Parsons, Kansas, home to Gunnery Sergeant Robert Carbon. The Gunny had been medically retired as a result of his wounds on the day that Christian died. He was recovering in his hometown with his wife and children as his support. Jason had not called ahead to say he was coming, but Marines did not have to do that. When you showed up on the doorstep of a Marine you served with in combat, you were on the doorstep of a brother, and he would always let you in.

Riding through the Ozarks on this bright autumn day was a truly freeing experience for Jason. The light of the sun, the golden leaves on the trees, the serpentine highway under his tires and the vibration of the engine occupied his thoughts and were an extremely therapeutic experience. Arkansas gave way to Oklahoma by early afternoon, and Jason gunned the engine through the hill country.

Rounding a corner, the loudness of his bike caused the horses in a roadside pasture to run. Jason appreciated the view: a large farmhouse painted white and set back from the road, the big red barn in the backyard, and silos in the distant field all reminded him of what he considered the true America. It was places like this that raised the families of patriots who always answered the call to arms when their country needed them.

It was not long before he crossed the Kansas border and headed toward the Gunny's house. Arriving in the driveway in the late afternoon sunlight, he saw the garage open and a late-model Ford Explorer parked inside with the hood up. As he shut off the bike's engine, he saw the Gunny look out from under the hood. He came around the vehicle, limping and using a cane with his left hand. Jason thought about the last time he had seen the Gunny - unconscious, barely breathing, blood covering his legs and face. He looked a lot better now but he was only a shadow of the burly Marine Jason had feared and respected during their year in Iraq.

A huge smile crossed the Gunny's face as he recognized Jason. "Hey Devil Dog, did you take a wrong turn on your way out of Nashville?" he barked.

"No Gunny, I just wanted to see what it's like for you now that you're living a life of leisure," Jason answered as they embraced.

The front door opened and a beautiful woman stepped out. She was tall with long curly brown hair that flowed over her shoulders. She wore tight blue jeans that accented her shapely figure, and cowboy boots that Jason did not doubt had shuffled across many a country bar's dance floor.

"Sergeant Broaduc, this is my wife Kirsten. Kirsten, this ugly goof is Jason Broaduc."

"Call me Jason," he said extending his hand to Kirsten.

Bypassing his outstretched hand, Kirsten grabbed him around his neck and held him tightly. "Thank you for saving Bob's life," she said as tears started to flow.

"I just did what anybody would have done," Jason said as she continued to hold him.

She slowly released Jason, keeping her left hand on his shoulder and wiping the tears from her eyes with her right. "I know better, and YOU know better," she said sternly. "Bob told me you could barely walk, but you went inside and found him anyway."

"All right, that's enough of that sentimental stuff," the Gunny said. "Let's go grab a cold one."

Jason was only too happy to sit in the shade of the back porch and sip a Budweiser with his old Gunny. "I heard you got the Silver Star," the Gunny said. "Congratulations, well-deserved. They gave Major Campbell the Bronze Star posthumously. He deserved more."

"Here's to the Major," Jason said as they toasted and took a long pull from their bottles. They sat in an oddly-comfortable silence for a long time after that. Each man watched the sunset, and remembered friends who would never toast again.

"So what's next for you?" the Gunny asked, breaking the silence.

"I start back with the highway patrol on the first of the month," Jason replied. "The hip still hurts from time to time, but it's not too bad. I got a new boss there. He's a grade-A asshole. Not sure how that's gonna work out. This fucker is so jealous of anybody else's success; he just fucks everybody who gets near him."

"Sorry to hear that. They medically retired me after I got out of Bethesda. I get around okay, but as you can see I have my third leg with me all the time." He raised his cane to emphasize his point. "The last good night's sleep I got was sometime before we left for Iraq. Sometimes I wonder if I'll ever miss another sunrise. Two or three hours a night is about it for me."

"I know," said Jason. "That's my story too. The shrink told me it would get better, but it's only gotten worse. I'm hoping once I get back into a routine at work it'll be okay, but I have my doubts."

"Well, what can you do?" the Gunny replied with more than a

hint of resignation. "You can't change the past, and the present never goes away."

"Yeah. I know." Another long silence ensued, and Jason went to the refrigerator and retrieved two more Budweisers. He sat down and realized that he was with one of the few men he could actually talk to about anything that happened in Iraq. Even when Jason spoke to other veterans, whether their theater of battle was Iraq, Afghanistan, Vietnam, or even old-timers from Korea and those few surviving servicemen from World War II, Jason found that he rarely spoke of the bad days. He could communicate that with only a look, and he understood the look in their eyes as well. Some things were better left unsaid. This man understood fully because he was in the same fight.

"Dinner's ready!" Kirsten called out to the porch from the kitchen. Both men rose slowly and moved inside to the table for a home-cooked meal, something Jason rarely got to enjoy. He found himself a little jealous of the Gunny. He had a beautiful wife who clearly loved him, kids who had a war hero for a dad, and he never had to answer to a boss again. Kirsten insisted that Jason stay a couple days, she instinctively knew that the visit was good for both men.

Jason ate well, and actually slept through most of the night. Iraq was being purged, and he felt better in the morning. The Gunny took full advantage of Jason's mechanical prowess that day. Jason replaced the water pump on the Ford Explorer, then they took it into town to buy a snow blower for the coming winter. "Don't think I can operate the shovel anymore since I have to use three legs now," the Gunny joked as Jason loaded the blower into the truck.

"Life of leisure," Jason smiled, closing the rear hatch.

Chapter 10

The next morning found Jason southbound from Kansas and passing through Oklahoma. There was still time before he had to return to work, and he wanted to let the open road work its healing magic. Nearing Texarkana, Arkansas, he spotted a dozen bikes outside an isolated bar that looked like it was in danger of collapse. A neon sign flashed Budweiser in the window. It looked like a good place to wash the road dust from his throat.

Parking near, but not too near the other bikes, Jason walked toward the door where two leather-vested men stood guard. Each had a rocker across the bottom of their vest backs that read "PROSPECT." Each was about Jason's age and had long hair and bushy goatees. They were large men, at least as large as Jason. As he approached the door one of them said, "This is a private party. You can come in, but there's a $20 cover charge."

"What's inside that's worth twenty dollars?" Jason asked as he looked at the one who spoke. No sooner had these words escaped his lips than the door burst open and a large, drunken, middle-aged, hairy man burst forth with a woman in tow. In tow meant he was dragging her by her hair, swearing as he went. He wore the full patch of the FOUR ACES Motorcycle Club, top rocker with the club name, a center patch with a poker hand of four aces held by skeletal fingers, and a bottom rocker showing the club's territory. In this case, the bottom rocker read "OKLAHOMA".

The woman he was dragging was in her 40's or 50's. It was hard to tell because the years had not been kind to her. Her face held deep wrinkles from too much sun, probably a result of untold hours spent on the backseat of a motorcycle coupled with too many cigarettes. Her hair was long, curly, and a shade of red that nature could never produce. She too wore a vest, and on the back it had two patches. The first read "FOUR ACES" and the second read "PROPERTY OF SMELLY."

Jason and the two Prospects stood aside as the duo passed into the gravel parking lot. As they went by, Jason inhaled and did not have to wonder who "SMELLY" was. "You dumb bitch!" Smelly yelled as he reached the parking lot and threw her to the ground. "If you want to fight somebody else's Ol' Lady, DO NOT pick the President's!"

She rolled up on her knees in the gravel. No tears came. She was far too used to this treatment. No doubt, she had endured much worse at the hands of Smelly and his club before. She was so drunk; she was even unsteady on her knees. "Fuck you!" she slurred. "You're gonna fuck that little whore and she wants it."

Smelly looked as if he would hit her, but gave up on the idea. She did not seem worth it to him. "Don't fucking come back inside. You can wait out here until the party's over. You ain't welcome back in."

He turned and looked at the Prospects. "Don't let that bitch back inside." Almost as an afterthought, he added, "But don't let her dumb ass out of the parking lot either. That drunk cunt will get run over on the highway." Looking back at her, he yelled, "...AND REALLY

RUIN OUR PARTY!"

The Prospects nodded. "You got it Smelly."

"Who the fuck is this?" Smelly asked, nodding his head toward Jason.

"Just passing through and stopped for a beer," Jason said.

"You like pussy?" Smelly asked him.

"The more the merrier."

"Well then get inside. Lotsa young pussy in there." Smelly led the way back into the bar and Jason followed, looking back over his shoulder at the disheveled woman still kneeling in the parking lot. Apparently the cover charge did not apply when a member invited you in.

Once he was inside, Smelly disappeared into the gloom and the cigarette smoke. Jason paused by the bar near the door and let his eyes adjust to the dimness. A jukebox along one wall blasted a David Allan Coe country tune. Two pool tables were in the center of the room next to a dance floor in front of a small stage for the occasional band. The FOUR ACES hardly noticed him as he ordered a Budweiser from the bartender, a pretty young woman wearing a bikini top and shorts that were a little too short.

Smelly was right. There were at least two women in the bar for every man. Many wore PROPERTY OF... patches, but most wore next to nothing. Clearly, the FOUR ACES had rounded up about half of the "talent" in the area for their party. Jason imagined that it was lonely in the topless clubs around the county because all the strippers were in this no-name bar as guests of one of the largest motorcycle gangs in the country. They danced all around the bar, flirting with the bikers and probably being well tipped for their efforts. Jason noticed that most of the women with PROPERTY OF… patches were sitting together in a corner and paying no attention to the men. This seemed routine for them. A few sat near their men, yet appeared just as interested in the dancers as any guy in the bar.

Taking a long pull from his bottle of beer, Jason felt sort of sorry for the women. All of them. The guys in this bar obviously respected none of them, and cared only for themselves and their fellow bikers. As he was thinking this and surveying the scene, one of the dancers approached him. "Why aren't you wearing your cut?" she asked, referring to the FOUR ACES vest all the others were wearing.

"Not in the club," Jason answered as he looked at her. She was about 19 years old, 5'5", and might have weighed 110 pounds soaking wet. A lacy bra was her only top and did little to cover her ample cleavage. Her shorts were baggy enough to display the top of the thong panties she wore. High-heeled shoes completed the outfit, such as it was. Her shoulder-length hair was dyed blond and parted on the side of her pretty face, highlighting her deep brown eyes. Her face revealed too much innocence to be caught up in a situation like this.

"Are you a Prospect?"

"No. Just came in for a cold beer. Seems like a happening party."

"Only the best for the FOUR ACES," she replied. "Would you like a lap dance?"

"Maybe later," Jason replied. "I just got here."

"Okay," she said, stroking his forearm with her hand and looking at him with a little girl's sheepish pout. "I'll be around whenever you're ready."

"Thanks," Jason replied. He could feel a swelling in his pants. He had not been with a woman since before being wounded. He honestly had not thought about it too much since then, and that was very unusual for him. Before he deployed to Iraq, he slept with different women on a regular basis. His work for the Tennessee Highway Patrol meant he was off duty at odd hours and on irregular days, so he bounced around from one woman to another throughout the week. They were all pretty, and they all understood that he was not there for a commitment. They appreciated his honesty, and he prided himself on the fact that he did not have to lie to get laid. "Chicks dig guys in uniform" was an old saying, and Jason had both his Highway Patrol uniform and his Marine Corps dress blues, "… making panties drop since 1775," as another saying went.

The jukebox began blaring a Motown hit from the Pointer Sisters. One of the FOUR ACES exploded, "I hate this fucking music! Who played this shit?" He glared at all the others, looking for the culprit.

"Hey Beaver," one of the others called him by name, "get over it. It's just a fucking song."

Beaver was middle-aged and overweight, but he lunged across the pool table at the younger man who had spoken. Stepping aside, the younger one dodged his drunken assailant and backed away as Beaver slipped from the pool table and fell to the ground. Everybody was moving now. The women were getting out of the way, while other club members grabbed Beaver and the younger biker, whose name patch read "RUBBER," to keep them apart.

Jason never moved from the bar. This was not his fight. It was FOUR ACE against FOUR ACE and they could handle their own problems. The irony of Beaver trying to get a piece of Rubber was enough to make him smile. He chuckled to himself, "It's usually the other way around."

While the FOUR ACES worked out their issues, Jason downed his beer, walked outside, fired up the Road Glide and headed deeper into Arkansas.

Chapter 11

Two days before his first shift back with the Tennessee Highway Patrol, Jason showed up at Headquarters to pick up his Explorer. The first thing he noticed was that it had not been moved from the spot it was in the last time he saw it, nearly a month ago. It was obvious that Captain Tucker had not done anything with it, as he had promised he would. In his office surrounded by his "I LOVE ME" memorabilia, the Captain looked at Jason with something between disinterest and contempt. "We've been busy, Trooper," he said as he opened his desk drawer and removed a set of keys. Tossing them to Jason, he said, "I didn't have the chance to get your vehicle serviced. It's got all the basics. I put in a request with the state to get a new car for you, but these things take a while." He was lying and Jason knew it. There would not be a new car in his future for a long time.

"Yeah, Captain. Thanks," Jason said barely masking his sarcasm. He turned to leave with the keys in hand. Pausing at the door, he turned back to the Captain, seriously thinking about confronting him right here and now about the screwed up situation he found himself in, and the fact that being effective in his job would be nearly impossible with the vehicle he was assigned.

The Captain looked at him incredulously. "Is there anything else, Trooper?"

Seeing the hopelessness of this situation, Jason bit his tongue. "No Sir," he said, closing the door to the office as he walked out.

Back in the parking lot, Jason turned the key in the ignition of the Explorer. Nothing. "Fuck me!" he yelled as he leaned back in the seat. He took a quick inventory of the dead SUV. An ancient radar gun sat in the passenger floorboard. "Probably hasn't been calibrated in years," he thought. "The first lawyer who challenges this relic in court is going to get his client off." There was no cage to separate prisoners from the front seat, no computer to get license plate and driver's license information. He would have to call in every traffic stop to dispatch, which not only took longer, but also was aggravating for both the trooper and the dispatcher.

Opening the door to the dispatch office, he walked inside to call for a service vehicle to jump-start the Explorer. He sat in the dispatch room while he waited. Lorye Williamson was the dispatcher on duty. She was a plump woman in her early 50's who had worked the radios for nearly 30 years. Jason liked her; she was a devout Christian and was always pleasant to everyone she met. "I'm so glad you're back safe and sound," she said. "My church and I prayed for you the whole time you were gone. When we heard you were wounded, we held a special prayer meeting just to blanket you in the grace of Jesus."

"Thank you," Jason said. "It must have worked because here I am. Good as new." He smiled at the gray-haired matron who cared for every trooper on the force as if they were her own sons and daughters.

"Praise Jesus!" she raised her hands toward Heaven. "Thank You Lord!"

"Listen," Jason began again, "the Captain gave me that old Explorer out back. There's no computer inside, so I'm going to be calling in every stop." Giving her a look that communicated how he felt about the Captain, he continued, "Y'all will just have to bear with me until he comes through with something better, but judging from my two encounters with him so far, I wouldn't expect that to be anytime soon."

"Don't worry about any of that honey," Lorye said. "That's why we're here. And Captain Tucker is going to come around. We pray for him every week at church too. We pray for all of you." She smiled as if she knew that her direct intercession with Jesus had saved countless lives. Jason did not know if he really believed in prayer or not, but he was sure that it could do no harm, so he let her go on. He knew her heart was in the right place, and he was willing to give her the benefit of the doubt.

The security camera overlooking the parking lot showed a state maintenance truck pulling up to the Explorer. Jason said, "Looks my rescuer is here." He stood to leave.

"Your rescuer is Jesus Christ and don't you forget it!" Lorye smiled as she gave him a hug. "You be careful out there Jason. There's a lot of people who love you."

Oddly, Jason thought, "I can only think of one person who loves me, and that's you." This caused him to feel a wave of depression as he exited the Headquarters building. "Love is not really a part of my life," he said to himself as he walked toward the Explorer. The deepening depression he felt at this made him physically shake his head to rid himself of the demons. Nothing seemed to help anymore.

Chapter 12

At 10 pm on Halloween, Jason adjusted his gun belt before getting into the Explorer for the two-hour commute to work. "First night back on the job," he thought. Nervous excitement filled him as he drove. Crossing the Dickson County line, he called on the radio that he was on duty. "Three Thirty-Three, welcome back," came the reply from dispatch. It was not Lorye's voice, but the voice of another dispatcher who was closer to 30 years old. Jason could not remember her name, but she was an attractive lady with a very short haircut and tattoos covering a significant portion of her body. She was divorced from an abusive husband, and could be a little surly from time to time, but she sounded pleasant enough tonight.

"Three Thirty-One, Three Thirty-Three." It was TJ, also on duty tonight, and Jason was happy to hear him. "Let's Signal Seven at the high school parking lot." This was code for, "let's meet at the high school parking lot and get caught up with each other."

"Ten-four," Jason replied. Halloween was a busy night for all law enforcement officers in America. It surpassed New Year's Eve for DUI arrests, and there were countless acts of vandalism and other crimes. This year it was a Sunday night, so most of the partiers had a head start on a night of drinking. Arriving in the parking lot, Jason saw that TJ was already there.

"Nice truck," TJ said as Jason pulled up beside him and turned the manual crank to lower his driver's window in order to talk.

"Thanks," Jason replied, sarcasm dripping from his voice. "That asshole really hooked me up. This piece of shit only has an antique radar gun that hasn't been touched in years. I don't even want to try and look for speeders. Anything I get from this gun would never hold up in court. I gotta try and get it calibrated later this week. Meanwhile, I have to hand-write all my tickets because there's no computer, so I'm pretty much fucked all around."

"Damn," was the only response TJ could muster.

"Where you working tonight?" Jason asked.

"South side. You?"

"West, I guess," Jason replied. "Nobody's told me shit. Just hoping it's quiet."

"On Halloween? Right! Good luck with that." TJ smiled and looked out toward the highway. "Haven't seen much of you since you got back. Whatcha been up to?"

"Took a bike trip for most of October. Went out to Kansas, and back down through Arkansas and Mississippi."

"Wow. That's cool. What's out there?" TJ asked.

"Nothing. Just riding 'cause I can," Jason replied, intentionally omitting the visits to Christian's parents and the Gunny. That was not a conversation he felt like having tonight.

"Okay. Well, I'm gonna head back down south and pull a drunk off the road," TJ said, putting his brand-new Charger in gear.

"Be safe," Jason replied as he waited for TJ to move. He rolled his window up as the big man pulled out onto the highway. He reestablished himself on the west end of the county when his radio crackled. "Dispatch, Three Thirty-Three, respond to Highway 70, mile marker one-eleven. Ten-forty six, single vehicle in ditch." This meant a car had run off the road and wrecked.

"Three Thirty-Three, Ten-Four," Jason said as he turned on his lights and headed toward the scene.

He arrived in less than ten minutes, and found a 1995 Chevy half-ton truck with the front end mangled by a culvert just past a curve. The driver was standing beside the road, and a car was stopped nearby with its warning flashers on. Jason positioned himself behind the wrecked truck and left his blue lights flashing as he exited the Explorer. "Is anybody hurt?" he asked, holding his flashlight on his shoulder as he approached the man.

"No," came the reply. "That's not my truck. I'm driving the car. I saw this when I was passing by and stopped to help. The driver took off running through the woods when I got out. He may be drunk, I don't know. He didn't say anything, he just took off. There's nobody in the truck. I called 911."

"Thanks," Jason replied as he shined his light into the truck cab. The airbag was deployed, and there was visible blood on it. He thought to himself, "These fools think they can get away, but they never do. I'll have him in custody before daylight."

"Are we done?" asked the man. "I would like to get home."

"Let me get your information, and then you can go. Can you describe the driver? Height, weight, hair color, clothes, anything?"

"Didn't see his clothes, but he's a white guy about 6 feet tall. I would say medium build. He was wearing a baseball cap."

Jason filled out the paperwork while he waited on a tow truck. At 3 a.m., he was on his way to the house of Mr. Reginald Hughes, the registered owner of the wrecked truck and the one likely to be in jail for DUI and leaving the scene of an accident before sunrise.

Reginald lived about four miles from the accident scene. As Jason pulled into the neighborhood, still about a mile from the address, he saw a man walking along the sidewalk. He was muddy and wearing a white baseball cap. Jason flashed his blue lights and the man turned to look at him. His face was bruised as if he had been in a fight and blood from a broken nose was still drying around his lips. Parking the Explorer in the street with the blue lights still flashing, Jason asked, "Are you okay?"

"I'm fine, Sir," came the reply. There was a slight slur in his speech. He was just under six feet tall, and lean. His orange T-shirt with the University of Tennessee logo on it was ripped, dirty, and had blood stains near the waist where it had been used to wipe the man's face.

"What happened to your face?"

"Nothing. Just goofing around." The man was clearly nervous, looking up and down the street. It was deserted at this hour, not even a light was on inside any of the homes.

Jason was standing on the sidewalk next to the man now. "Can

I see some ID?"

"Sure." He reached into his back pocket as Jason took a cautious half-step back with his right foot to shield his state-issued Sig-Sauer .357 semi-automatic while keeping his flashlight on the subject. Producing a wallet, the man nervously fumbled around in it, and pulled out a driver's license.

"Reginald Hughes," Jason read aloud. "Mr. Hughes, do you own a 1995 Chevrolet pickup truck?"

Knowing he was busted, Reginald turned and began running down the sidewalk. Jason caught the smaller man in less than ten feet. Grabbing his collar, Jason snatched him backwards onto the ground. The man struggled, but it was useless against the larger and much stronger state trooper. "That wasn't very smart," Jason said as he rolled Reginald onto his belly and began handcuffing him.

"Fuck you asshole!" he yelled. "I'll have your badge for this!"

"For what?" retorted Jason as he lifted the handcuffed man to his feet. "Arresting you for DUI, leaving the scene of an accident, and resisting arrest?"

"Fuck you!" he slurred one final time as Jason placed him in the backseat of the Explorer.

Processing Reginald into the county jail took the rest of Jason's shift and then some. He was not finished with all the paperwork until after 9:00 in the morning. On the drive back home he thought to himself, "I get to do it all over again at midnight tonight."

He managed only three hours of fitful sleep before the alarm woke him and he left to return to the job. Midnight shifts were the worst, and he was scheduled for five in a row. The Captain really had it in for him, and it was obvious that this treatment was going to continue until either Jason or the Captain was gone. As the junior trooper in the division, Jason was not even eligible for a transfer for at least another year. "Can I take it that long?" he thought to himself on the long drive back to work. "Fuck it. I took a year in Iraq; I can take a year of this moron's shit. How bad can it be?" This thought steeled him through the next three shifts.

Returning home from his fourth consecutive midnight shift, he was bleary-eyed from lack of sleep and the general stress of non-stop work. The radio crackled with a message to report to the division office to see the Captain. Jason acknowledged the call then pulled out his cell phone and dialed the Captain's office number. "I need you in my office ASAP," was the only reply the Captain gave. It did not sound promising, and in his anger, Jason pulled a sharp U-turn in the middle of the highway, bringing looks of shock and surprise from the driver behind him and a man working in his yard nearby. The world turned slightly red as Jason sped away toward Headquarters.

By the time he reached the Captain's office, his anger had cooled somewhat and he was again in control of his faculties. Stepping into the room with all the prized photographs displayed on the walls, he stood in front of the Captain's desk. Again, the Captain hardly acknowledged Jason's presence, focusing instead on the obviously "very important" paperwork in front of him.

Finally setting it aside, he looked at Jason. "There's a special detail we've been asked to assist with in Greene County," the Captain began. "Some sort of Joint Drug Task Force bust, and agencies across the state will be in on it. They only requested one trooper from us, and you're the one. I really don't have any more details than that, but you need to be at the Greene County Sheriff's Office at midnight tonight, where you and everybody else will get the brief."

"Sir, I just came off four midnight shifts, and Greene County is 300 miles east of here. I will have absolutely no chance to get any rest before this thing kicks off. Are you sure there's nobody else you can send?"

The Captain looked extremely stern, but Jason could see he was enjoying this. "Trooper, you have your orders. Be there tonight. This is not open for debate." A smug smile crossed his face. "I thought you Marines were supposed to be tough," his voice condescending now, and Jason felt a flash of anger he was certain the Captain saw. He turned and walked out of the office without another word. "That motherfucker is gonna get his ass kicked one day," he thought to himself as he exited the building."And I hope I'm the one who gets to do it."

Chapter 13

The Greene County Sheriff's Office looked as if it were hosting a law enforcement convention. The parking lot overflowed with Crown Victorias, Dodge Chargers, blacked-out Suburbans, and one small Ford Explorer with the Tennessee Highway Patrol logo on its door. "This is the worst patrol vehicle in the state," Jason thought to himself as he crossed the lot and entered the office complex.

Inside was a large conference room filled far beyond capacity. Federal, state, and county officers crowded in and huddled in small groups. Jason did not know any of them. Most were in uniform, but there were several in plain clothes. These were the leaders and the federal agents in charge of the operation. "Gentlemen," one of them spoke from the front of the room. He was a very physically fit man in his mid-forties, wearing black cargo pants and a black polo shirt with a badge embroidered on the left breast and DEA in big letters across the back. "I'm Special Agent Hamermill, and I will be giving you your assignments. Tonight brings to a close a joint operation that has been ongoing for nearly two years. We will be serving federal arrest warrants on nearly 100 suspects across three counties in relation to trafficking in methamphetamine, crack cocaine, prescription drugs, and of course, marijuana."

"I would like to introduce you to Special Agent Tyler," he

continued as a man with long, dirty, stringy blond hair stepped forward. "He's our undercover agent whose work has made tonight's operation possible. He's been working these suspects from the very beginning, and I would like you all to give him a big round of applause."

All the officers clapped gratuitously. Their hero simply smiled and sat back down. He looked like he had been on drugs himself. Even from his post in the back of the room, Jason could see the exhaustion in the man's eyes. Undercover work was tough, requiring long hours and many dangerous circumstances. If his cover was ever blown, he was as good as dead. Add to that the fact that he still had to build strong cases and collect evidence that targeted not one, but dozens of individuals simultaneously, and the workload became more than most men could bear. That created enormous stress and this guy clearly needed a break.

Agent Hamermill finished briefing the operation to the gathered forces. When the assignments were handed out, Jason saw that his role was about as unsexy as it could be in a bust like this. When the order to move was given, he was to block one street corner near a drug dealer's house so the federal agents would be free to go in with the warrants and arrest the suspects without anyone coming or going unexpectedly.

Everyone was positioned over the next few hours so the warrants could be served simultaneously across all the counties at 4 a.m. Jason's position was in a small middle-class neighborhood in Leesburg, on the outskirts of Johnson City.

Precisely at 4:00 in the morning, the radio crackled with the word to move. Jason turned on his blue lights and pulled into the middle of the street. He stood beside the truck with an M-4 rifle, and had an uneasy feeling. Iraq. Vehicles. M-4s. This was all too familiar. He tried to shake the thoughts, but could not. A car approached from down the street. Jason's world turned red. He was immediately back in Al Rubtah. He saw the vehicle bomber approaching Staff Sergeant Aranda … Jason raised the rifle and yelled, "STOP! STOP NOW OR I'LL KILL YOU!"

Terror filled the man's eyes and he sat still with both hands on the steering wheel. "I don't understand," he yelled out the window. "What did I do?"

Jason lowered the rifle. He suddenly realized where he was and what he was doing. Only then did he recognize that the driver was a thin black man in his 60's. Shaking his head to clear the cobwebs and breathing heavily, he said, "Just stay in your car for a few more minutes, Sir. This road is blocked and you can't come this way."

"I'm on my way to work," the man said, the fear still in his eyes. "I work at the bakery on Garden Avenue."

"You can't come this way," Jason replied, more relaxed now. "If you want to turn around and take another route, that's fine, but this road is closed."

Without another word, the man started the car, put it in reverse, and pulled away. "That sucked," Jason thought to himself as the taillights disappeared down the street. "He probably thought so too."

No other vehicles approached, and by 4:30 a.m. Jason was driving the nearly 400 miles back to his home in Paris.

It was nearly dark when Jason pulled back into his driveway after crossing the length of Tennessee for the second time in a day. He had not slept for nearly 48 hours and was exhausted. He showered and lay on his bed, but sleep would not come. Anger and despair boiled inside him and he could not turn it off. Flashes of Iraq, Captain Barnes, Lance Corporal Smith, and the old black man from this morning roiled in his mind. He held his .45 in his hand as he tried to fight off the demons, but nothing helped. Around midnight, he got up, opened a beer and sat on the couch in the dark slowly drinking it from his left hand while he cocked and un-cocked the .45 with his right. Click. Click. Clack. Click. The hammer made the sounds again and again.

Click. Click. Clack. Click.

Click. Click. Clack. Click.

Click. Click. Clack. Click.

As the sun rose, half the beer was still in the bottle, flat, warm, and stale. He poured it into the sink, and put on his leather jacket. It was cold, probably in the thirties. "Maybe a motorcycle ride will wake me up," he thought as the Road Glide came to life in the garage.

The cold air stung his face and hands as he roared up Highway

641 towards Kentucky. He had no destination, just the need to be doing…something…anything…anything but sitting in his dark house with a stale beer and the demons that would not leave him.

In Murray, he turned onto Highway 94 and rode east toward Hopkinsville. By 9 a.m., he was in Aurora, a tiny map dot on the shores of Kentucky Lake. He needed gas, so he stopped at the town's only pumps and filled the tank. The station not only served as the town's sole source of fuel, but also as the lone source of groceries, and the post office. While Jason was filling the tank, several muddy pickups were in the parking lot with their drivers all dressed in camouflage from the morning's deer hunt. It was opening day for deer season, and was observed by the locals as a holiday second only to Christmas. The men, along with their sons and even a couple of daughters were generally engaged in admiring the few who were successful from the hunt. They eyed Jason with suspicion as he clearly stood out from the crowd. "Where you from?" the clerk behind the counter asked as he paid for his fuel. She was young, about seventeen, and attractive. "Her dad probably owns the store," Jason thought to himself as he watched her making change for the twenty. She had several earrings in each ear, and too much makeup. He could see in an instant that she wanted to get out of this one-horse town at the first opportunity. She was underdressed for the weather, with a tank-top shirt and blue jeans with holes strategically ripped in the legs.

"Tennessee," he replied.

"What brings you out here?" she continued, wanting to keep the conversation with him going, because he was the only person within fifty miles who was willing to discuss something other than today's dead buck, a subject she clearly had no interest in.

"Just out for a ride," he said. "Enjoying the day."

"Melonheads Bar is across the street," she offered. "Sometimes bikers stop there, but mostly in the summertime. Don't see too many bikers after it starts to get cold." She was twirling her straight, shoulder-length, brown hair with one finger, trying to be enticing. Jason again felt that twinge in his pants, but instantly reminded himself that she was too young. He shook off the feeling, but he had to admit that it was a cold morning, and a quick shot of whiskey at Melonheads might just warm him up.

"Thanks. I might go over there for a few minutes."

Inside the bar, the air was dark and stale, smelling of cigarettes, old beer, and dust. Jason let his eyes adjust for just a minute, then walked to the bar. The few customers this early on a Saturday morning were obviously old local alcoholics. Three men and one woman sat at the bar, while two other men sat at a high table near the dartboards. The bar stools were all covered in duct tape, and no two chairs at any table matched. Jason could tell that the owners here quit caring about the furnishings years ago and determined they would just keep selling beer and whiskey until the place collapsed. After that, they would sell it for scrap lumber and live out their days in the doublewide house trailer down the road.

"What'll it be?" asked the bartender. She was a large woman about sixty years old, and Jason pegged her immediately as the owner, or perhaps the owner's wife. She was dressed in an old, wrinkly Harley Davidson T-Shirt, stained and faded sweatpants, and a pair of worn-out Crocs. Her hair had not been brushed since yesterday, and she clearly could not have cared less.

"I'll have a double shot of Jack," Jason answered, surveying the rest of the crowd. As the woman poured his drink, the men at the bar nodded to him, and the woman at the end of the bar smiled. She was probably in her mid-forties, but she looked like she was closer to sixty. She wore a white tank-top men's undershirt and faded blue jeans tucked into her aging cowboy boots. Her face was haggard from too many smoky barrooms, and the paint on her nails was chipped and gouged from inattention.

As the bartender set Jason's drink in front of him, he laid a $20 bill on the bar. "Thank you," he said as she went to fetch his change.

"You're welcome," was the reply as she walked toward the register without looking back.

The man closest to him at the bar was already drunk, and looked at Jason from a stooped position over his half-empty draft beer. "Where you from?" he slurred.

"Tennessee," Jason replied for the second time in less than five minutes.

"Cold morning," the man said as Jason downed the whiskey in one swallow. He immediately felt the warmth rush through him. Lack of sleep, job stress, and too little food were taking their toll. He was suddenly aware that he felt relaxed for the first time in months.

"Sure is," Jason answered holding the empty glass in the air toward the bartender. She grabbed the bottle off the shelf and walked toward him to provide the refill. She was not back with his change before he was ready for his third drink.

"Better slow down, honey," she said as she filled the glass again. Jason pulled two more twenties from his wallet and slid them across the bar.

"I'll be fine. Let me buy a round for all my new friends."

"Hear, hear!" shouted a couple of the patrons as the bartender went about filling their glasses. One of the men at the bar took his fresh beer and walked down to Jason. "Thank you," he said. "Name's Carl Evans." He extended his hand toward Jason, who shook it firmly. He was surprised by the man's grip, and he noticed the dirty ball cap the man wore. It was emblazoned with a Marine Corps emblem underneath the words "Vietnam Veteran."

"Semper Fi," Jason replied as he released the grip.

"Semper Fi," Carl replied, a surprised expression on his face. "Who were you with?"

"Second Civil Affairs Group. Just came back from Iraq in June."

"Welcome home!" Carl exclaimed and slapped Jason on his back. "By God, it's good to meet another Marine! Lucille, get this man another drink! He's home from Iraq!"

Applause broke out across the bar, and Jason enjoyed his first real hero's welcome. Everyone toasted and cheered him. "Welcome back!" and "Thank you!" were shouted time and again. Another round of drinks appeared, and Jason began to sip rather than gulp. He still had a long ride ahead, and he was already feeling numb. "All things in moderation," he thought as Carl sat on the stool next to him. When the initial celebration waned, a serious look came across Carl's face. He leaned close and Jason could smell the beer on his breath. In a voice only slightly above a whisper he said, "Jason I've been at this a long time, and I have seen that same look in the eyes of a thousand young Marines fresh out of the 'Nam. I've had that same look myself, and I wish I had someone to point this out to me when I was just back. Son, you look like shit. When was the last time you slept?"

The power of Carl's candor stunned Jason. He felt like he should lash out at the old Marine, but the look in Carl's eyes was of pure pity, not judgment. Carl felt Jason's pain, and he obviously knew what he was talking about. The seriousness of the moment sobered Jason instantly.

"I haven't slept in a long time. In fact, I can't even remember the last time I slept through a night."

Carl's look of empathy deepened. "I know how that feels. Listen, when I first got back, there was no hero's welcome. Nobody wanted anything to do with us. I gotta tell you that I didn't handle it well. I got into the bottle, into pot, into just about anything I could to try and forget the 'Nam and the things that happened there. Spent some time in jail, then spent some time in prison. Look, I ain't proud of the things I did after I got back, but I'm pretty straight now. I drink some beers every day, and I been on Social Security disability for about 10 years, so I don't work. I'm really no good to anybody anymore, but maybe I can do some good if I can get you not to end up like me."

The look in Carl's eyes hardened, his voice became a hoarse rasp, and the volume increased, but not enough to be heard over the juke-box by the others. "Don't let these demon bastards get the best of you! You can still beat them!" His expression was now one of near-fury and his voice rose another octave as he half-yelled, "Don't end up like me!"

Jason recoiled from the jolt of emotion he felt. Carl was standing, poking a finger in his own chest over and over yelling, "Don't end up like me! Don't end up like me!" Carl's friends came to his side, and took him by the arms, walking him backwards towards a chair. They had seen this behavior before, and knew how to help their friend. Jason backed out of the bar into the sunshine and cool air.

The coldness on his face only sobered him more and he thought to himself, "I gotta get outta this place." The Road Glide thundered to life and he pulled away heading towards The Trace, a winding two-lane highway running south through Land Between the Lakes and back towards home.

Storm clouds were closing in and dark was settling early as he pulled into his garage. Exhausted, he peeled off his clothes and took a long hot shower. The steam was soothing and melted the stresses away for a moment. Collapsing into the bed, he slept the kind of sleep that was known only by those who had truly reached the limits of human endurance. When the morning came, he was the most relieved man in the county. A full twenty-four hours before he had to be back at work, and he was actually well-rested.

The rainstorms of the night before continued through the day. Jason used the time to take care of some household chores, then sat back with a cold beer and turned on the TV for an afternoon of NFL football. Life was back in perspective.

Chapter 14

It was 7:58 a.m. when Jason radioed into dispatch alerting them he was on duty. He had been on the road towards Dickson County for ninety minutes, but he was in a good mood. That was shattered when dispatch called back that he was to report to Captain Smith. Jason knew this could not be good news.

Thirty minutes later, he pulled into the parking lot at Headquarters and shut off the engine. The dispatcher on duty was a new girl Jason had not met. She was in her mid-twenties, with long brown hair and green eyes. Her red blouse barely contained her breasts, and her skirt showed very shapely legs and a pair of firm buttocks even while she sat in the chair. She looked nervously at Jason as he passed by.

Captain Smith was standing behind his desk when Jason walked in the office. There was no pretense of superiority and making Jason wait while he tended to meaningless paperwork. The look on his face was of pure fury, his eyes were piercing, his cheeks flushed, forehead and eyebrows furrowed into a deep V. "What the fuck happened in Greene County?" he howled. "Some poor old black man is telling anyone who will listen that a crazed trooper nearly killed him last week! You better have a good fucking reason for what went on, or your ass is gone, Trooper!"

Jason felt his own anger rising, but felt helpless to control the situation. That desperation only made his temper boil even more. He restrained himself and said, "My orders were to keep traffic off the street. This man was coming towards me, and I did what I had to do to stop him. He went away, and the operation went off without a hitch. What more do you want?"

"What more do I want?! What more do I want?! I'll tell you what I want! I want my troopers to be able to get a 67-year-old bakery worker to turn around and go in a different direction without sticking a rifle in his face and threatening to kill him. That's what I want, but since I clearly can't have that where you are concerned, here is what I'm going to do."

He reached down to his desk, lifted a plain white envelope from it, and extended it toward Jason. "This is a three-day suspension without pay. You're lucky this is your first offense and there were no witnesses. I would love nothing more than to fire your ass right now, but I have to follow procedure. When you come off suspension, you will be working straight graveyard shifts starting Thursday until I say stop. You will be on from midnight to 8 a.m. Thursdays through Mondays. All the other troopers who get to sleep with their wives and girlfriends because you are covering their shifts say 'Thank you.' Now get out of my office, and don't fuck up again. You are on a VERY short leash, and I will not hesitate to can your sorry ass if you so much as misspell a name on a traffic ticket." He sat down and looked at some papers on his desk. Jason turned and left - there was nothing more to do for the moment.

Winter passed into spring, and Jason finally worked his first day shift since his suspension in November. He was totally burnt out, but he had managed to keep his nose clean. The one benefit of working graveyard shifts was that he never saw Captain Smith. As the months had worn on, his fellow troopers were very empathetic with his situation. None of them liked the Captain. They tolerated him when they had to, and avoided him whenever possible. Jason knew he was not alone, but he still felt like the bastard held a singular grudge against him.

On a bright, sunny, warm Saturday morning in April, Jason radioed dispatch that he was on duty at 8:00. The return call was not the usual "Ten-Four," but "Proceed to the intersection of Highway 49 and State Road 235 to handle a Ten Forty-Six with possible fatalities."

With his blue lights flashing and the siren wailing, Jason drove the Explorer as fast as it would go. As he parked in the middle of the street, he assessed the scene. He saw the remains of a small gray Saturn straddling the shoulder of the highway. The rear half of the car was nearly ripped apart from the front half. A 1970's model Ford pickup truck was nose-down in a pond about 100 feet away. The front of the pickup was mangled, but the sturdy construction of the older vehicle kept it mostly intact.

Climbing out of his vehicle, Jason noticed several people near the Saturn. A middle-aged Hispanic male was frantically trying to get into the rear end of the car. An Hispanic female, in her thirties, and her daughter, approximately 10 years old, were nearby. The woman was on her knees in the middle of the road wailing and screaming hysterically, "Mi bebe! Mi bebe!" The daughter looked almost catatonic as she stood on the shoulder of the highway watching all this unfold before her. As Jason approached, he could see a child, about two years old, still strapped into a safety seat in the back. Clearly this child had taken the full impact of the Ford pickup, and the entire side of the car was folded over on top of the seat. Blood and brain matter were pouring across the toddler's face, and his small body was totally crushed from the impact.

Muscling his way past the family, Jason quickly recognized that there no way the child was alive, but he carefully reached through the wreckage and gently checked for a pulse. Sirens could be heard in the distance, and he knew the rescue squad was on its way. Looking up at the father, Jason saw total desperation in the man's eyes. "I'm sorry," Jason said, shaking his head. The man fell to the ground next to his wife and together they wept with a bitterness unknown to most.

Turning to the daughter, Jason checked her over and found only a few superficial cuts on her left arm and leg. She stared blankly at her parents as Jason sat her down on the shoulder of the road. With some difficulty, he then guided both of the adults over next to their daughter before turning his attention to the other vehicle as the rescue vehicles pulled onto the scene.

The driver of the Ford was standing on the road near his truck and did not have a scratch on him. "Are you all right?" Jason asked as he approached the man. He was in his mid-fifties with a potbelly, and leathery skin that comes from years of working in the fields. His arms were large and he sported faded blue tattoos from under the rolled-up sleeves of his flannel shirt. He wore a greasy cap with the word "Copenhagen" on the front. Gouges and stains on his steel-toed work boots showed years of wear.

"I'm fine. I don't know what happened," he answered. Even from arm's-length Jason could smell the stale beer on the man and see the glazed look in his eyes. Another man standing nearby stepped up to the scene and said, "I was behind the family in the car. This man ran the stop sign and hit them square. He was flying. If he hadn't hit them, he still would have ended up in that pond. This is a nightmare. What the hell were you thinking, mister?" he asked the man.

"I don't know what happened," the man repeated.

"Sir, have you been drinking?" Jason asked.

"I was just…I was at my friend's house last night. I was going home." He looked like he was in shock, but it was hard to tell if it was the crash or the booze. Jason sat him down on the side of the road and said, "Wait here." He then pulled his portable Breathalyzer out of the Explorer and returned.

Administering the test, he got a reading of .22. He administered it again just to be sure and got a .23. "You are under arrest for DUI and vehicular manslaughter." Handcuffing and lifting him from the ground, Jason placed him in the backseat of the Explorer and put a seatbelt on him so he could not easily move. Before he even got back to assist the rescue personnel, he looked over his shoulder and the man had passed out.

More units were arriving and the sheriff's deputies began directing traffic. All the while, the husband and wife wailed so loudly that it haunted everyone there. Nothing could console them over the loss of their son. The daughter still stared blankly as if she were no longer present. Her body was on the scene but her mind was in some other parallel galaxy.

As the rescue squad cut the side of the car away with the Jaws of Life, Jason began the accident reconstruction. Using the physical evidence and eyewitness accounts, he determined that the initial story was true. The family in the Saturn were westbound on Highway 49 when the Ford driven by a man with nearly three times the legal limit of alcohol in his system ran the stop sign at State Route 235 at over 50 miles per hour and T-boned them. The rear driver-side door where the two-year-old boy was buckled in his car seat took the entire impact, ripping the Saturn nearly in half and sending it careening sideways up the highway.

Jason returned to the Saturn just as they were lifting the child from the backseat. The family was all in an ambulance, but the woman's screaming had not abated. Jason wondered how she even had a voice left, but she clearly would not be consoled. As the ambulance pulled away with the entire family inside, an eerie silence fell across the scene. Tow trucks and clean-up crews began their work, and Jason transported his prisoner to the county sheriff's office for processing.

The paperwork and getting the man booked into jail took almost all day. Jason could still hear the woman's screams in his head as he handed the man over to the jailer. With less than an hour of duty left, he considered just sitting at the station, but decided to wait near the county line on Highway 70 and check for speeders before he headed home.

He found a shady spot to park and thought, "I shouldn't even turn my radar on." He smiled to himself and sat for several minutes before he picked up the radar gun and actually hit the "ON" button. "Ya'll are gonna have to be going pretty fast if you want to meet me today," he said to the passing cars. He really did not want to do any more work.

With only about ten minutes left on his shift, he saw a car approaching faster than he had seen in a long time. The radar chirped 102. Jason flipped on the blue lights and pulled out behind the car. "If he wants to outrun me, he won't have much trouble," he thought. "I'll never catch him in this piece of shit." The car did not run, however, and pulled over less than a mile up the road. As Jason approached the rear of the brand new Cadillac DTS, the man in the driver's seat rolled down his window and started cursing. He was wearing a turban, and had a full beard and mustache of black hair. He was wearing a very expensive-looking suit and had a Rolex watch among other gold and diamond jewelry. "What the fuck?" he screamed in perfect, unaccented English. "You fucking pigs are always profiling me! I am NOT Muslim! I am Sikh! Why did you stop me?" he demanded.

"Sir, you were going 102 miles an hour in a 55 mile an hour zone."

"Fuck you! You fucking lie! I don't give a fuck what you say, you fucking jackass. I was NOT going that fast."

Jason bit his tongue and restrained himself. He was already burned out, stressed out, and worn out. He was not going to be sucked in by the man's tirade. "Sir, I need your license, registration, and insurance."

The man thrust the documents out the window. "I don't have to take this shit! I am a very successful businessman and just because I wear a turban, every stupid-ass redneck cop in the South thinks I'm a terrorist. I'm NOT!"

Jason grasped the documents and turned back to his patrol vehicle to write the ticket. Despite trying to remain calm, he was seething. He could actually arrest this guy for going that fast, but that would mean another three hours of paperwork. He was just going to write a ticket and let the man go.

Returning to the car with the ticket in his hand, he gave the driver back all his paperwork. "This is fucking bullshit!" the man yelled. As Jason turned to go back to the Explorer, the driver sneered and said "Allah fucking Akbar motherfucker."

The world went red. Turning toward the driver, Jason reached through the window and grabbed the man's shirt collar with his left hand. Pulling him out through the window, he landed three hard right fists to the man's face and head before was he even completely out of the car. On the ground, with Jason on top of him, the man was barely conscious as Jason landed blow after blow to the man's face. "Fuck you motherfucker! Fuck you!" Jason said as blood spattered across the man's coat, the side of the car, and the pavement.

A passing motorist saw the fight, stopped, and got out. "Everything all right?" he asked as he ran up. Jason quit swinging and looked up. He saw his surroundings clearly for the first time in several minutes. The man lying underneath him was unconscious and almost unrecognizable through all the blood. His turban lay a few feet away, and his shoulder-length black hair was soaking in his own blood and spit. Two of his teeth jutted loosely through his cheek.

Another motorist stopped and announced she was calling 911 for an ambulance. Jason stood and looked down at the man. This was not good.

Within moments, a deputy pulled up, and for the second time today, Jason could hear the sounds of an ambulance siren in the distance. As the deputy stepped out of his car, he looked at the scene before him in horror. Jason knew him from having crossed paths at accident scenes and other minor dustups during the last several months. His name was Clyde Burrow and he was 29 years old. Born and raised in this county, he had been with the sheriff's department for over five years. He enjoyed his work, but nobody could enjoy the scene that was before him now. "Jason, are you okay? All you other people get back! Step out of the road before you get run over!" He was waving his arms at the small crowd to motion them away. As they stepped aside, he took Jason by the arms and led him to the front of the Explorer. The ambulance was pulling onto the scene as well. Jason felt stunned, he leaned backwards on the front of his vehicle and watched the ambulance crew get out and start tending to the injured man.

"You're bleeding," said Clyde. Jason looked down at his hands where several of his knuckles were cut from impacts with the man's head. The front of his uniform was spattered with blood as well. Clyde produced a handkerchief. "Wipe your face," he said. More blood spatter came off on the cloth. "It looks like except for your hands, it's all his blood."

Jason still said nothing. "What the fuck happened here?" asked Clyde.

"I don't know. I wrote him a ticket, then he must have said or done something to set me off. My God! I hope he lives."

"Me too," responded Clyde.

Chapter 15

J ason spent the wee hours of the morning typing up his report
from the traffic stop and beating the previous afternoon. Rather
than leave it in the computer and report to duty he printed it and
waited for the Captain to come in. He knew there was no pretending about this. He had made a very serious mistake and he was going
to have to pay. The Captain still had not shown up, so Jason waited
with the dispatcher. It was Lorye.

"Jason, I am so sorry to hear about what happened yesterday,"
she began as he sat down. "I can't imagine what you must be feeling.
I know that fatalities of children are always the hardest, especially
when it was a DUI. Then to have to fight a man on the side of the
road, that must be awful. You look like you haven't slept at all."

Jason stared at the computer behind her and said, "No. I haven't
slept in a long time."

"Everybody's talking about the fight yesterday" she said. "Some
of them are saying it was unprovoked, but I told them all to keep
their mouths shut. They have no business second-guessing anything
until the report comes out, and they know it." Jason knew that Lorye
would keep the gossipers silent, but that could only last so long.
When this report came out, there would be plenty to talk about.

Captain Smith walked past the door to the dispatch office and down the hall to his own. "Well, I guess I better get this over with," Jason said resignedly.

"Honey, I'll be praying for you. You just tell the truth. No matter the consequences, the truth will always set you free."

Captain Smith took his time reading the report while Jason stood in front of his desk. "This is very serious," was all he said.

"Yes sir. I know."

"Okay. Well, I will have to talk to my boss about it, and he will have to talk to his. There's no doubt this is going to be a big black eye for the whole state. I wouldn't be surprised if the governor himself had to comment on it. One thing I am sure of is that this guy is going to sue as soon as he gets out of the hospital. You're damn lucky he's not dead."

For the first time ever, Jason saw a look of concern, or was it fear?, on his Captain's face. "You need help Jason. I'm referring you to our department shrink. I want you to wait out in the front while I set it up. I'll have you in to see him this morning."

This morning turned out to be 3:00 in the afternoon. After a full day of sitting in the undecorated room where troopers did their paperwork, Jason was at his wit's end. He was bored, depressed, and quite angry by the time Captain Smith walked in and gave him the address of a doctor's office in town. "He can see you at 4:00," and with that, he left the room.

The psychologist's office was nicely furnished. Overstuffed leather furniture and a cherrywood décor made the place comfortable and welcoming. It reminded Jason of a cigar bar, only without the tobacco and booze. Dr. Hammond welcomed him with a big smile. He was middle-aged, a little soft around the middle, and dressed in a sport coat but without a tie on his button-down shirt. His round face looked larger because of the baldness on the center of his skull.

Jason sat in a comfortable chair. "Not a couch," he thought to himself, and realized he must have spoken it out loud when the doctor chuckled and said, "No, but we can get you one if you like."

"No thanks Doc. I'll be fine" he replied with a strained smile on his own face. The doctor took the seat across from him, opened a manila folder and pulled reading glasses from his coat pocket. Perching them on his nose, he looked over the top of the rims and said, "I understand you had quite an unusual day yesterday."

"That's the understatement of the year."

"Do you want to tell me about it?"

"Do I have a choice?"

"Of course you have a choice, Jason. I'm not here to make you uncomfortable, although I realize that this is difficult. I'm not here to judge you, and I assure you that I won't. I'm just here to let you tell me whatever is on your mind. If you're uncomfortable with something, just don't say it. My assessment is strictly a fit for duty or not fit for duty. The details of what you tell me will remain solely between you and me. No one from the department, or any judge, or anybody anywhere will ever have access to these files. When we're done here, I'll write a report that analyzes nothing except your need, if it even exists, for further treatment and counseling, and your ability to perform as a Tennessee Highway Patrolman."

Jason thought about this. He was angry, depressed, had not experienced a good night's sleep in months, and was constantly anxious and stressed. The smell of the leather furniture, the warmness of the office, and the candor of the doctor told him this was safe. He talked for an hour about the events of the previous day, and the doctor listened. When it was over, Jason drove home feeling like a giant weight had been lifted from his shoulders.

When he got home, his answering machine was blinking. It was Captain Smith. "Jason, I'm sure you knew this was coming, but you are suspended indefinitely with pay until this matter is cleared up. Call me if you have any questions."

———— ≫))⟨⟨(◯)⟩⟩≪ ————

The matter was cleared up the following week. Jason reported to the Captain's office, and both the Captain and his boss were there. Jason knew this had to be bad. The newspapers were alive with the story of the beaten man, and several lawyers were jockeying to take his case and sue the state of Tennessee. The man had already undergone two surgeries, and at least two more would be necessary to repair the multiple fractures, replace lost teeth, and reconstruct his ruined face.

Captain Smith began, "Jason, that beating is going to cost the state millions. In cases like this, the patrol has to take swift and decisive action. The shrink diagnosed you with Post Traumatic Stress Disorder. Even without that diagnosis, we would still have to act, but with the diagnosis in hand, we have no choice. PTSD and law enforcement don't mix. As of this moment you are terminated."

It hit him like cannonball. He suspected this was coming, but to actually have it delivered in such a nonchalant way made it all the more difficult to hear.

The Captain's boss spoke up. "Jason, there is a good chance your PTSD came from your time in Iraq and not your time with the patrol or somewhere else. You were wounded in action, for God's sake. I recommend you go contact the Department of Veterans' Affairs. Not only can they provide you with help, medications, whatever, but you will probably get a disability check from them as well."

Jason was still stunned. He set his state-issued pistol and his badge on the Captain's desk and left without uttering a word. As he exited the building, both TJ and Lorye were in the parking lot. The sadness on their faces spoke volumes and Lorye was dabbing a tear from her eye. "Jason, I am so sorry this happened," she said. "I would give anything to turn it around." Hugging him, she added, "I'm going to keep praying for you, and you're always welcome to call anytime you need anything."

TJ put his hand on Jason's shoulder and said, "Let me give you a ride home."

During the drive, he and TJ discussed the situation. Jason took the negative tack: newly unemployed, no prospects for making a living, diagnosed with a disorder that was totally screwing up his life, he felt more alone than ever. TJ listened empathetically, and just before he reached the Paris city limits, he made a suggestion that gave Jason hope.

Jason did not know if it would work, but he at least knew where to begin. No sooner had TJ pulled out of Jason's driveway, than Jason got on his bike and left. He knew he needed some help, and on TJ's recommendation, rode straight to the local Veterans of Foreign Wars lodge. Surely the guys at the VFW could point him on the right path with the VA.

The VFW in Paris, Tennessee, was a run-down building just off the courthouse square. Its primary function was as a bar, a place for all the old guys to gather and drink while they told their war stories. Jason had never been inside, but when he entered, he was the only one there except for the bartender. It was dimly lit and smelled musty. The seat cushions were poorly maintained, and tiles were missing from some spots on the floor. Walking up to the bar, Jason ordered a Budweiser. "Not too crowded in here today," he said to the man opening the longneck bottle.

He was old - at least 70 - with leathery skin, scarred hands, and a big handlebar mustache. White hair flowed haphazardly from under his red VFW cap. His piercing stare suggested he had seen the worst of the world and nothing was going to surprise him this late in life. "Son, it's noon on a Wednesday. If you want a crowd to drink with, this is neither the time nor the place."

"I'm sorry. I didn't mean it to sound that way. I'm actually look-ing for some information. I need to contact the VA to file a claim."

The old man's deep, icy, blue eyes went soft. Jason was staring at a man who shared an inner pain only brothers could feel. Pain brought on by uniquely terrifying moments, and a lifetime of living amongst a public that could never understand. Pain that was doubled by the guilt over lost friends, men too young to die, but dying brutal and horrifying deaths worse than anyone deserved. This man understood Jason in an instant, and Jason understood him. Pushing a booklet across the bar, he said, "This has every number for everything the VA does. If it ain't in there, then the VA don't do it."

Jason looked at the booklet, A Veteran's Guide to the Veterans' Administration. He put it in his pocket, thanked the man, and left.

"If I didn't have PTSD before, I damn sure would now," Jason said to the first human he could talk to at the VA. He had spent two hours locked in a computer-phone hell, pressing one button for one option and another for another. The spokesperson apologized, and asked how she could help. He explained what he needed.

"We'll send a packet of claim forms to your house. Fill them out, and mail them back. We'll let you know our decision as soon as we can."

Chapter 16

As April turned into May and then into June, Jason remained unemployed, living off what little was left in his savings account. He got his first and second notices from the mortgage company that if he did not resume payments on his home, they would be forced to begin foreclosure proceedings. He needed a break, so he climbed on his bike and headed south. There was no destination in mind; he just wanted to get out of Tennessee and away from the depression for a while.

Georgia was hot and humid in early June. On the highways south of Henry, the heat danced off the pavement in waves. The air was heavy with the smells of the countryside, every field burgeoning fatly with its crops of corn and soybeans. Even the bugs seemed fat and lazy as they crawled or flew around the roadside parks and primitive campgrounds Jason stayed in night after night. He was riding aimlessly, staying on the back roads and two-lane highways, just generally avoiding crowds and civilization. For two entire weeks, he pored over the southern parts of Georgia and Alabama, then headed into the Florida panhandle and spent another week sipping Budweiser and watching the waves roll in onto the pure white sand beaches.

It was nearing July, and he decided to point north again and see if Tennessee was any less depressing now than it had been when he left. He stopped for the night in Atlanta and booked a room in a seedy hotel in the northern part of the city. It was Friday and the local bar down the street was gearing up for a big night. Jason showered and changed, then walked into it for a burger and a beer. The place was brighter on the inside than it had been on the outside, and Jason took a seat in a booth because all the barstools were taken. A friendly young waitress was at his side in less than a minute. "Can I get you something to drink?" she asked.

"Sure, I'll have a bottle of Budweiser and a cheeseburger."

"No problem, honey. I'll have that right out for you." She sashayed away toward the kitchen in blue jean shorts that were cut so high they would not have covered her panties, even if she had worn any. Her tee shirt was tied under her small but firm breasts. She was not wearing a bra either.

When she returned with the bottle of beer, it was fresh from the cooler, ice cold and dripping wet. She leaned over and set it on a coaster, and Jason could see her breasts with their small pink nipples in the front of her shirt. "I haven't seen you in here before," she said as she stood and turned to the side. She rested her left butt cheek on the edge of the table, and Jason could see the flatness of her abdominal muscles.

"Nope. I'm just passing through on my way home." He took a long pull from the beer as he said this, looking her in the eye. The cold shocked his mouth and he noticed ice crystals intermixed with the liquid. "This may be the coldest beer I've ever tasted."

"Yep. Coldest beer in Georgia. That's our claim to fame." She smiled as she spoke. Her teeth were perfect, and she wore little makeup. She did not need any. "Where's home?" she asked. Her gray eyes were the perfect match to her complexion and Jason could feel a warmness in his groin as she spoke.

"Tennessee," he replied and took another long drink from the bottle. "How about you? Born and raised in Atlanta?"

She giggled slightly and her eyes were alive. "No, I'm from South Carolina, but I'm going to grad school at Mercer. Getting my MBA, then who knows where?"

The small bell in the kitchen rang, signaling that Jason's burger was ready. She returned with it and another Budweiser. The crowd ebbed and flowed through the night and Jason was comfortably settled in as he drank a few beers and talked to Kristina "but everybody calls me Kris" until closing time. She walked back to the motel with him. "I love your motorcycle!" she said as they walked in front of it to the door of the room. "Can I come in?" she asked, with a smile and a look that said there was only one answer to this question.

———◦《◦》◦———

The sex was powerful, animalistic, and everything about it was perfect. The sweat of their bodies mingled and the grunts and noises of ecstasy resounded off the walls. When it was over, they lay next to each other, their naked bodies touching, and fell asleep within minutes.

Jason awoke from another nightmare only an hour later in a cold sweat. His heart was pounding and his head hurt. It took him a moment to adjust to his surroundings. The bedside clock read 4:12,

Kris was still sleeping soundly, and there were noises from the street in front of the motel. Something was out of place, and Jason rose from the bed and put on his blue jeans. Retrieving the .45 from the nightstand drawer, he tucked it into the small of his back and looked out the window. Three black men were by his bike. One of them sat on it and was trying to roll it backwards.

The chain on the motel room door snapped when Jason snatched it open and confronted the men before him. He hit the closest one with a roundhouse right that knocked him to the ground. The motorcycle fell on its side as the one atop it jumped off and ran toward the street. The third man came forward, but Jason caught him by the throat with his left hand. Pulling the .45 with his right, he stuck it under the man's eye and held him against a pole supporting the covered walkway in front of the room. "Motherfucker I will kill you right now!" he snarled. The fear in the man's eyes was electric. He could not breathe with Jason's iron grip on his throat, and his feet barely touched the ground as Jason held him pinned against the post. A small trickle of blood came from under his eye where the pistol barrel cut him.

Jason heard movement behind him, and turned, still holding the man by the throat. The first man he hit was staggering to his feet, but was still wobbly from the punch. Jason threw the man he was holding into the other and both fell to the ground again. A spotlight and blue lights from the street lit up the scene. As the Atlanta police officers skidded into the parking lot, Jason lowered the pistol to the ground.

Two men were lying on the ground next to bike that was on its side. Jason stood half-dressed on the walkway with the pistol at his feet, and Kris appeared in the door with the bed sheet wrapped around her. She was scared and confused at the melee. The two officers pulled their pistols and ordered everyone to lay face down. All four complied, and they handcuffed everyone but Kris.

More units pulled onto the scene, and when it was all over, the two black men were arrested for attempted theft, and Jason was arrested for assault and brandishing a firearm. He protested that he was only protecting his property, but the cops were not listening. Apparently, it was just easier for them to arrest everyone and let the judge sort it out.

The cell in the Atlanta jail was cold at 8:00 in the morning after the fingerprinting, booking, and obligatory mug shots. Jason shared it with three young Hispanic males who had been arrested the night before. Whites and Mexicans could be housed together in Atlanta, but blacks were always segregated. That might have tempered the physical violence, but the verbal threats, assaults, and abuse were alive and well after everyone got their breakfast of ice-cold eggs, grits, toast, and lukewarm coffee that looked and tasted like dirty water.

An argument was raging through the cell doors as different gangs tried to prove their superiority. Jason's cellmates were all from one gang, the North Street Familia. They were yelling at some Crips down the hall, and the Crips were yelling at some Bloods further down the hall. The Bloods were yelling at everybody, and Jason sat in the corner of the cell and listened to it all through a pounding headache. One of the North Street Familia members, probably a leader, threatened to kill any Crips he saw on his turf. "I'll shoot your black ass on sight motherfucker!" he yelled. "Don't come down on North Street unless you're ready to die, bitch!" His head was shaved and tattoos covered his entire scalp. Only his face was untouched, and Jason suspected that was next on the list.

A guard came down the hallway and yelled for silence. It was marginally effective, and the uproar subsided enough for him to open Jason's cell and say "Mr. Broaduc, the magistrate has declined to press charges. Come with me; we'll get your belongings and you'll be free to go."

Jason stood and the North Street leader said "Sure, let the white man go. I see how it is."

"Shut up Julio" replied the guard. "You do your time and let everyone else do theirs. And knock off all this bullshit down here or the next time you see me I'll be taking you to solitary."

Julio rolled his eyes and walked to the back of the cell. "Whatever Vato."

Chapter 17

The decision from the VA came in the middle of the July, three months after he lost his job with the highway patrol. The letter was just as coarse and impersonal as Captain Smith had been when he fired Jason.

Sergeant Broaduc,

We have reviewed your claim for disability compensation for Post Traumatic Stress Disorder (PTSD) dated 22 April 2005. Nothing in your personnel file or military medical records indicates you were ever diagnosed with this disorder while on active duty. There is simply no way to substantiate whether the events resulting in your diagnosis of PTSD by Dr. Hammond on 8 April 2005 were caused by traumatic events occurring as a part of your role in the Marine Corps or your role in the Tennessee Highway Patrol. Therefore, the VA must deny your claim.

Jason threw the papers across the room. This was total bullshit. Abandoned by the federal and state governments he swore to protect, the governments he repeatedly fought for, he felt a sense of loss for everything he had ever cared about. "I only wanted to be part of a brotherhood," he thought. "Now what? Football? Gone. Marine Corps? Gone. Highway Patrol? Gone. I tried to serve something bigger than myself. Now I have nothing. And nobody."

Alone in his house on that hot night in July, he opened a beer and read the other letter that came in the mail while he was in Georgia. This one from the mortgage company, a foreclosure notice telling him to vacate the property by September 1st. "Barely five weeks away," he thought. He was furious at the VA, the Highway Patrol, and the bankers.

Walking through his garage, he spotted the box of his things the Marine Corps had returned to him. Opening it, he began sorting through its contents. The unmistakable odor of Iraq emanated from inside, and he saw again the blood-stained flak jacket and the bulletproof plate with five AK-47 rounds embedded in it. His other uniform items were clean and neatly packed inside. He held his K-Bar fighting knife, the one Marines had used since WWII, and it felt good in his hand. His boonie cap was stained and salt-encrusted from gallons of sweat. In the bottom was a small envelope with several photos. Thumbing through them, he spotted one of Muhammed Ali Banji, the Kuwaiti national who melted captured weapons. Immediately, a thought crystallized in his mind. Closing the box, he hurried back into the house, and found the small green notebook with the information from operational briefs and contacts from his tour in Iraq. Inside, he found the cell number for Muhammed.

Chapter 18

The next morning, Jason awoke early and fired up the motorcycle. He had spent several hours the night before calculating his plans. A few stars needed to align, but he could help manipulate them somewhat. Riding west, he crossed the Mississippi River near Dyersburg and stopped at the first Wal-Mart he came to in Kennett, Missouri. There, he paid cash for two cell phones and some calling cards.

As he crossed into Kentucky on Interstate 57, he stopped at the first rest area and parked in a back corner away from all the other traffic. He called Muhammed's number, and was relieved when he answered on the third ring. "Muhammed, this is Jason. Remember me from last year?"

"Allah be praised! Yes! Jason, I remember you! It has been too long, my friend. Where have you been?"

Jason took about 90 seconds to share the high points of his wound and that he was back in the states. Then he asked, "Muhammed, does your cousin still run that spice exporting business?"

"Yes, he does. He is doing very well, all praise be to Allah. Why do you ask?"

"I want to buy some spices," Jason answered.

—◉—

After the phone call ended, Jason dismantled the phone and stuck its various parts and pieces in his pockets. As he rode through southwestern Kentucky on his way home, he threw one piece at a time over every bridge he passed. No one would ever be able to trace that phone or that call.

Arriving back at his house, he packed his bag for another road trip. This one would take him right back to Atlanta.

Chapter 19

Riding south back towards Georgia the next day with his .45 tucked into the small of his back, Jason continued to evolve his plan. He still had some money in savings, but not enough to save his house. The house was not his real concern though. He had lost every job he ever had, and he needed some sort of stable income. Nobody was lining up to hire a disgraced ex-trooper with PTSD, and his options were limited.

When he arrived in Atlanta, it was nearly dark. He rode the motorcycle to North Street, and traveled its entire length. During that ride, he saw everything he needed to see. Stopping at another nondescript motel on the outskirts of town, he paid cash for four nights. He honestly did not know how long this would take, or if it would even work, but he knew it was his best shot at some sort of income for the foreseeable future.

The person he needed to see was not expecting him. In fact, Jason did not know if he could even find the man, but he knew where he needed to look. There was a six-block stretch of North Street he rode through the day before where every store sign was in Spanish. It was a depressed area with dirty sidewalks, and many young thugs walking the streets among an older population that came here looking for a better life but never found it.

About 5:00 the following evening, Jason left his motel and headed back to the neighborhood. When he arrived, most of the merchant shops were closing for the evening, a clear indication that a different clientele roamed the streets after dark.

In the time since he lost his job, Jason kept his head shaved, but began to grow a goatee. It was now nearly long enough to braid. He wore his motorcycle boots, old blue jeans with his .45 tucked in the back, and a tank-top t-shirt from a Harley dealer. He still performed an intense exercise routine several days each week. This kept him in top shape and his arms, chest, back, and legs bristled with sinewy muscle. He looked like a biker because he was a biker. No loyalties held him to anything anymore.

He spent the entire evening wandering from one cantina to another, into and out of topless bars and pawnshops, looking for his man, but never saw him. Jason was a patient hunter; he learned that first from his father and later from the Marine Corps, so he was not discouraged. Arriving back at the motel at 4:00 in the morning, he hung up the "Do Not Disturb" sign, closed the curtains against the coming sunrise, and slept soundly.

This pattern repeated for two more days. Jason saw several members of the North Street Familia, but none of them was the one member he needed. They were easy to identify by the black bandana tied around their right bicep. Jason persisted in his hunt, patiently waiting, knowing Julio would surface sooner or later. He knew better than to ask around, because aside from looking like a biker, he could easily be mistaken for an undercover cop. The wrong comment to the wrong guy about Julio could send him and the other gang leaders underground for months, foiling the whole plan. No, Jason needed to see Julio personally, and he was willing to wait for that.

He paid cash for two more nights at the motel. As the days wore on, his patterns changed. He spent more time in the North Street Familia's turf, and watched their activity more closely. It was clear that the marijuana trade was strong here, as he had witnessed dozens of transactions on street corners and in alleyways during his search for Julio. It appeared most of the people involved in the sales were young men in the country illegally. They needed the money, and dealing drugs for the North Street Familia represented quick cash and little danger. Jason rarely saw a patrol car in this area of town. The Atlanta police probably were not too concerned with a bunch of illegal aliens who rarely left their neighborhood.

Jason ate in the local restaurants and had become quite accustomed to a diet of fish tacos, burritos, and pico de gallo. He drank Budweiser with his meals, and always watched and listened. The customers and owners spoke Spanish exclusively with each other. He could order in English or Spanish, but always chose English. A white man with a Southern accent who ordered in broken Spanish could easily be mistaken for an undercover cop or INS agent trying too hard to blend in with the local surroundings.

As he sipped from a bowl of shrimp gazpacho for dinner in a restaurant so small it could easily have been a converted storage closet, Julio walked in with two other Familia gang members. They looked like his bodyguards. The owner, a Mexican in his early fifties, greeted him. "Buenos noches! Como esta' tu?" he asked.

Julio's reply was, "Bien. Gracias, mi Tio'! Y usted?"

The conversation continued in more Spanish that Jason did not understand, but he had some vital information. The restaurant owner was Julio's uncle, and Julio respected him.

As Julio left, Jason followed and called out to him about a block down the street. "Julio!"

Julio and his two henchmen stopped and turned around. "Who are you?" they asked. Each had the trademark black bandana on their arms, and another pulled across their foreheads and covering most of their eyes, so they had to tilt their heads back to see.

"We did a little time together in Atlanta lockup a few weeks ago," Jason said to Julio.

The looks of suspicion grew deeper on all the Mexicans' faces. "So? What's that got to do with anything?" he asked.

"While we were there, you threatened to kill any Crips or Bloods who came down to North Street. I happen to know those guys are nationwide, and if they did decide to come down here, you couldn't do much about it. I have an answer for you, but we need to go somewhere that's private so we can talk."

"Fuck you Vato!" one of the henchmen spoke up. He was only about 18, but already had the jailhouse tattoos of a veteran. "We only deal with people we know! And you? We don't know you."

Julio spoke up. "I remember you Vato, but that don't mean anything. For all I know, you're just a cop who was put in there for show. You got sprung pretty quick. Why should I do business with you?"

"Because I have access to exactly what you need if you really want to protect your turf from the Crips and Bloods. You know you don't stand a chance with just your throwaway nine mils. You need real firepower, and I can get it."

Julio looked intrigued. "Why should I trust you? How do I know you won't be selling to those guys too? Why do you want to help us?"

"The short answer is that you need the guns, and I need the money. You got a good thing going here. Pot, crack, meth, and women, but you need to protect them. You can't do it with what you got."

⸻◦⟨◉⟩◦⸻

Later, in the basement of a crack house, the deal was made. Ten totally untraceable AK-47s at $500 each. Flown into the Atlanta airport and labeled as spices. The uncle's restaurant would be on the shipping label, and a couple of North Street Familia's mules would pick them up from the cargo area at the airport. Jason used the second cell phone he bought in Missouri to call Muhammed and arrange the details, then destroyed it just like the other.

Chapter 20

A week later, Jason was sitting on his bike on a hilltop outside Atlanta. He was with two members of the North Street Familia. Everyone was silent and the air was tense. This thing could blow up at any second, and they all knew it. Nobody trusted anyone. A cell phone rang in a Mexican's pocket and everybody jumped. It was the first sound they had heard in an hour and it was deafening and scary. He spoke quickly in Spanish then turned and looked at his cohort. Nodding, he walked up to Jason and reached into his back pocket. Despite the heat of the early August evening, Jason wore a leather motorcycle jacket with deep front pockets. His .45 was in one and he cocked the hammer as the Mexican pulled out an envelope and smiled. "Julio says to be here with the same deal next month." Handing the thick envelope to Jason, he and the other walked toward their car and left without saying another word.

As they pulled away, Jason rode off in the opposite direction. He had $5000 in his pocket, but he had sold more than AK-47s. He had sold his soul. He was no longer just a disgraced cop and a war hero who had fallen on hard times. He was an international arms dealer who, after paying Muhammed his share via Western Union, made $4000 in profit for 10 rifles that were captured overseas and meant for the melting pot.

Back home, Jason packed the few items he wanted to keep be-fore they repossessed his home. He rented a singlewide trailer on a small lot halfway between Paris and Camden. It had an old and dilapidated shed that served well as a garage for his bike. He fur-nished the trailer with the bare essentials and left the keys to his soon-to-be-repossessed house with the bank on the day before they came to take over the property. Riding away from his childhood home for the last time, he decided he needed a beer. There was a bar near the highway about a mile from his new trailer. He noticed it the first time he went to look at the property, and saw that there were a couple of bikes parked out front, so he decided to try it. With a name like Ape-Hangers, how bad could it be?

It was early afternoon, and there was just one bike parked out front. Jason backed into a spot across the parking lot from it and walked through the main entrance. The building looked a little run down on the outside, but was reasonably clean on the inside. The lights were on, and it was bright. A small TV behind the bar aired the Discovery Channel, and the bartender sat on a stool staring at the screen. He was a large man in his mid-fifties and wore a motor-cycle vest with a three-piece back patch. The top rocker read IRON KINGZ. The center patch was a grinning skull wearing a crown and riding a chopper out of the flames. The bottom rocker read TENNESSEE. There was also a smaller patch with MC on it. Jason knew this stood for Motorcycle Club, and set these guys apart from most other bikers. When the man turned toward Jason to take his order, Jason noticed the front of his vest was adorned with numerous patches including "1%er", "PRES", and his road name: "LEX".

"I'll have a bottle of Budweiser."

The bartender did not speak but reached into the cooler and pulled out a brown bottle that was slippery from the cold. He set it on the bar as Jason slid a $20 bill across. When the man returned with the change, the door opened and two other bikers wearing IRON KINGZ vests came inside with two young, thin, but not very attractive women. Each of the women wore a back patch on their vest that read PROPERTY OF IRON KINGZ.

The men were young, probably no older than Jason, and he recognized one of them as a high school classmate. "What's up Lex?" yelled the first one through the door. He was skinny and had long hair pulled into a tight ponytail that hung past his shoulders. He was not a big man, but his wiry frame moved fluidly across the barroom floor.

"What's going on boys?" Lex responded.

"Ready to get our drink on," said the second man, the one Jason recognized from high school. Ricky Collins had dropped out of school when he failed to pass his junior year. This surprised no one, since Ricky had only come to school about two days per week for the last half of the year anyway. He had discovered a taste for marijuana, and spent most of his time trying to get it or sell it so he could get some more. Now, eight years later, he had smoked enough dope to fund a small nation. He was known around town as a small-time hood, basically just working, stealing, or otherwise earning enough money to keep the marijuana in his system and his worn-out bike on the road. Jason had not known he was a member of the IRON KINGZ, but that came as no surprise.

Jason's knowledge of the IRON KINGZ was pretty basic.

They were a local 1%er club that was made up of a few small time hoods like Ricky and a smaller number of legitimate citizens. Jason thought to himself that Lex must be on the border between the two. Legitimate bar owner, but president of a club that almost certainly had dirty hands.

"Hey Prez, we need to talk," the first man said in a lowered voice. His name patch read RATCHET, Ricky's read STONER. "Wonder how he got that one?" Jason smiled to himself. Ricky was so burnt out that he would never have recognized Jason anyway, but Jason looked very different from his days at Henry County High School. His head was shaved, and his goatee was now braided and hung past the neck of his Harley t-shirt. He was still extremely fit, typically doing several hundred pushups and sit-ups every week, but with his tank-top tee and his old blue jeans and motorcycle boots, he was a long way from the clean-cut citizen and high school jock that Ricky would have remembered even if he had enough brain cells left to do so.

Stoner looked concerned as the three men huddled at the far end of the bar and spoke in muffled tones. The two women sat at the other end of the bar and stared at the television. Jason could only hear bits and pieces of the conversation, but the gist of it was that Stoner had been robbing a house with another thug who was not in the club. The homeowners came home, caught them, and as the two men ran from the house, the husband shot and wounded the other man. He was arrested but Stoner got away, and the men were now worried the cops would press the accomplice hard enough to give Stoner up.

When their conversation was over, Lex looked angry, Stoner looked worried, and Ratchet was clearly ready to "get his drink on."

And that is exactly what he proceeded to do. Sitting down next to his young girlfriend, he ordered a beer and a shot for himself and a beer for her. Stoner took his beer and walked out the back door, obviously ready to roll a joint and escape his life. His girlfriend ordered her own beer and slid $2 across the bar. The last dollar was in quarters, clearly all she had, but she needed to escape too.

As the afternoon turned to evening, more IRON KINGZ came in, some with their women, some without, but all on their motorcycles, and all wearing their patches, nearly a dozen in total. Jason did not realize it when he first showed up, but tonight was church night. The night of the weekly club meeting they called church. Around 7:00, all the members disappeared into a back room leaving only one man other than Jason out front. This guy wore a vest with only a bottom rocker on it. It read PROSPECT. Church was a members-only event, so the Prospect looked after the bar while the club met.

Less than an hour later, the members filed out of the back and began to party in earnest. The Budweiser was flowing, and it was a raucous atmosphere. Music played on the jukebox, both pool tables were constantly in action, and some of the women were dancing. Jason, a little buzzed from the beers, was actually enjoying himself for the first time in a long time. Aside from the fact that the club members mostly associated among themselves, he spoke to a few and enjoyed the ongoing motorcycle discussions.

The one thing that was obvious was that these men loved each other and would do anything for one another. They were a family, and could never be accepted outside of the society they created for themselves. Most of these guys did not make much money, and rode bikes that were old and in constant need of repair. A few rode newer bikes, but Jason's 2004 Road Glide was the newest bike in the parking lot by at least four years. Many of the bikes still had kick-starters, and all were individualized for their rider. Paint, chrome, and accessories were different on each one, and Jason looked at them all before he left the bar.

Chapter 21

Every month, Jason visited a different store and bought a new burn phone. Every month, he used it once to call Muhammed and arrange another shipment, then destroyed it and scattered the parts around the countryside. Every month he rode his bike to Atlanta. If the weather was too bad, he drove his old Jeep, but every month, he was there. Every month he wired $1000 through Western Union, and every month he collected $5000 from the North Street Familia. His life revolved around these trips. Sometimes he would see Kris, other times he did not let her know he was in town. He needed to be off the grid, dealing only in cash, having few close ties with anyone. No one outside of Muhammed and the North Street Familia knew his business, and he knew his freedom and survival depended on it staying that way.

As winter passed into spring his goatee was now 10 inches long and braided into two strands with a black bead at the end of each; he was happier than any time he could remember. The IRON KINGZ had become friendlier and he was granted Hang Around status. It meant he was a friend to the club and was the first step toward membership. He drank with them several nights each week in the bar owned by their president, and he knew them all by name. Of course, that meant only their road names. The names given to each rider on the day he was patched-in and became a full member. Lex,

Ratchet, Stoner, Baldy, and the rest of the members only referred to each other by road names.

One evening while the action at the bar was uncharacteristically slow and quiet, Jason spoke to Lex, who was taking advantage of the lull in business to drink heavily from his own supply. "How did you get your road name?"

"Well, that's usually not something we talk about with non-members" Lex slurred, a little unsteady on his feet. "But I like you Jason," he slapped Jason on the back with a meaty paw, "so I'm gonna tell you." He lifted a glass of beer and finished it in one long drink.

"I prospected for the IRON KINGZ back in '78," he began. "Back then, there was no Tennessee chapter, and there were only five members in Florida. That was the whole club." He wobbled a little and leaned against the bar for support. "Let me tell you, those were some lean days, man! Anyway, I was only twenty-four years old, but I was already pretty much bald. Runs in the family, bad hair genes, I guess" he smiled as he rubbed a calloused hand over his slick head. "Most of the guys have long hair now, but EVERYBODY had long hair back then. When I patched in, one of the guys wanted to call me Kojak, but he was a cop on a TV show and the President said we couldn't have no members named after cops. So the movie Superman was just coming out, and somebody suggested Lex Luther, Superman's arch enemy. It just stuck, and I've been Lex ever since."

"Thanks for telling me, Lex. I guess you should be glad Wonder Woman didn't come out til later", he and Lex both shared a laugh.

———◦((○))◦———

Occasionally, members from other chapters would come in for a day or two. They were always welcomed like long-lost family. On a cool evening in early March, three men Jason had not seen before came in wearing their IRON KINGZ patches. At first, it was like any other visit from a distant chapter. These men wore bottom rockers that read DELAWARE. Two of the men were much older than the third, who looked younger than Jason. Their hair was long and gray, just like their beards. They were overweight, wearing dirty clothes, and their tattoos were both numerous and faded into bluish-black ink spots that bore little resemblance to whatever they represented when they were fresh.

The third man's head was shaved, except for a small patch at the base of his skull from which sprouted a long, thin, braided ponytail. His beard was also braided and matted from lack of care. His clothes were greasy, and his eyes carried a wild look that Jason knew instantly was the product of methamphetamine use. His name patch read "RAT", and the mind did not have to travel very far to see the resemblance between this skinny, hyperactive biker and an actual rodent.

They chatted with Lex and the other club members while the beer flowed. A few local patrons stopped in as well. There was never a shortage of young women in the bar, hoping to catch the eye of a club member. The Ol' Ladies tolerated these intruders with a quiet disdain. Some bikers were totally faithful to their women, but some really did view them like the PROPERTY OF... that their patches proclaimed. They would drink and dance with the unattached women right in front of their wives or girlfriends. Jason never appreciated that level of disrespect, but club business was club business, and none of it was his business.

Rat was sitting next to Jason at the bar about 9 p.m. The meth had worn off, and he was settled into just drinking beer. A local man Jason had seen before, but who was not in the club, entered the bar. He was wearing a shirt that proudly proclaimed US ARMY. His hair was short, and Jason knew he was in the local National Guard unit. The tattooed dispatcher from the highway patrol, whose name Jason still could not remember, was with him. She was wearing tight jeans and a shirt that enhanced her ample cleavage. Her hair was cut short on the sides, as if by a razor, and was dyed and spiked with streaks of pink on top. She reminded Jason of a punk-rocker.

They took two seats at a table and ordered draft beers from an Ol' Lady who acted as a waitress when things got busy. Some of the club members were playing pool nearby. A local member named Lefty was already drunk and he staggered around the table trying to line up a shot. Jason thought that must be difficult when you were seeing double. As he leaned over the pool table, he hit the soldier in the back of his head with the cue.

"Whoa dude! Take it easy!" the soldier said.

Lefty turned and glared at the younger man. "Just who the fuck are you talking to?" he asked.

"Look man, I don't want any trouble. Just be careful with the cue."

"I'll do whatever the fuck I want with this cue. In fact, I might just break it off in your ass soldier-boy!"

The situation was tense. Most of the club members had abandoned their conversations and were watching the argument unfold. The soldier was no more than five feet from Jason and he was getting nervous fast. The odds were against him when he was facing an entire club of bikers looking for a fight.

Taking the girl by the hand he said, "All right, look. I'm sorry. We're leaving. Have a nice night."

Stepping closer, Lefty said, "Maybe you will, and maybe you won't. It's our bar and our rules and you just broke rule number one: Don't fuck with us in our bar."

"Hey man, I'm not looking for trouble." He moved the girl behind him to keep her away from the bikers. She was almost in Jason's lap; he could smell her perfume, mixed with fear stemming from the danger that surrounded them.

There was a clear path along the bar toward the door, and most of the club members were willing to let them leave, but they knew they had to back up Lefty, and if a fight broke out, it would be all of them on this one soldier. Those are just the rules in the brotherhood of outlaw bikers. Nobody else in the world would lift a finger to help them, so they stick together and help themselves.

As the soldier began to back himself and the girl toward the door, Lefty continued to press the issue. He was getting closer, and the soldier was directly in front of Jason. His girlfriend was in front of Rat. In a flash, the soldier pulled a semi-automatic pistol from his hip. Just as fast, Jason caught his hand and took it away, then grabbed the man by his neck with his left hand and shoved him facedown into the floor. Pinning him to the ground with his knees, Jason held the pistol away from him with his right hand. It happened so quickly, no biker had moved. The girl screamed and began to sob.

"It's okay guys!" Jason yelled. "There's no reason for anybody to get hurt!" He picked up the soldier and whispered, "I'm going to walk you out, and you and your girlfriend are going to leave and never come back here again." The soldier nodded resolutely; he was embarrassed by the defeat, but was glad he was alive and able to leave.

The club cleared a path as Jason escorted the pair out, stunned by the speed, certainty, and brevity of the struggle. The IRON KINGZ were tough men who had been in a lot of fights, but they had not witnessed so quick a disarmament and so dominant an end to a fight that easily could have turned fatal.

Outside, Jason told the soldier, "I'm going to unload your pistol, keep the bullets and put it in your car trunk. You are a dumb motherfucker to do what you did. If I hadn't taken your gun, they would have, and they would either have shot you or beat your dumb ass to death with it. Don't come back here."

As the soldier opened the door to his Toyota, he said to the girl, who was now recovering from the shock of the situation, "Get in. We're leaving."

"No we're not," she replied in a tone that shocked even Jason. "You're leaving, but I'm staying. I'm not going anywhere with you again! This is only our first date and you nearly got us both killed." She grabbed her purse off the back seat, and added "I'll get a ride home from one of these guys. Don't bother calling me."

As he roared away in total humiliation, she turned to Jason and gave him a sultry look. "Buy me a beer?"

He looked at her closely. She was no more than 5'6", and although she was shapely, no one would think she needed to diet. Her pounds were well proportioned. "I'm Jason," he said extending his hand.

"Julie," she said, and she shook it gently in when the light of recognition dawned in her eyes. "Jason Broaduc?" she asked.

"Yeah."

"You look so different! What are you doing here?" Her voice lowered to a whisper. "Are you undercover?"

Jason looked at her sternly. "No. I don't do that sort of thing anymore. I'm just a biker."

"Well what do you do?"

Jason leaned in close to her and gave her a look that left no doubt about his seriousness. "What I do is none of your fucking business. It doesn't concern you or anyone else in the bar. Now if you want to come back inside, you need to know how to keep the outside world on the outside. Nobody's gonna ask you how you make your money, and you need to keep all that to yourself. The club's rules are all that matters inside those doors, and when you come in, you obey or get hurt. That's just how it is."

Julie looked a little apprehensive, but she was obviously attracted to this outlaw and the lifestyle. Glancing over her shoulder at the bar with a few IRON KINGZ standing in front, she asked coyly, "Are you gonna buy me that beer or not?"

As they reentered the bar, the expressions on the club members' faces were priceless. A raucous laughter rose across the bar as the IRON KINGZ realized that not only had Jason proved his dominance in the fight, but now he had the soldier's girlfriend on his arm. They looked at him with a newfound respect.

Taking his seat at the bar with Julie next to him, he ordered two beers. Rat was still on his stool, and he said to Lex behind the bar," I'll cover those beers." Turning to Jason he said, "Nice work. I was in the Marine Corps for four years, and I never saw anything like that."

"Semper Fi," Jason said, smiling. "I was in the Corps too."

"Who were you with?" asked Rat.

"Second CAG. Got wounded in Iraq, and got out"

Rat looked at him closely, as if he was studying every feature, and it was coming to him slowly through his beer and meth-induced haze. "Were you in Walter Reed?"

"Yeah," Jason said, looking closely at Rat. "How did you know that?"

"I was there too. Summer before last. I was hit in the shoulder in Afghanistan."

"Ray?" Jason said as the light finally dawned.

"Yes! Are you the guy with the Silver Star?"

"Yeah, that's me," he said, smiling broadly. "Small world, huh?"

"Oh yeah!" Rat exclaimed. He turned to the bar, and yelled out "Hey guys! Turns out me and this guy were in the Marines together!"

That brought a round of cheers. Since nobody at the bar ever discussed their past or their business, very few knew Jason had been a Marine. A couple of the club members came over and introduced themselves as former Marines also. Jason enjoyed talking with all of them, and by the time Julie climbed onto the back of his bike, they were both feeling pretty good.

Following Julie's directions, he rode toward Camden and pulled onto her street near the high school. She had rubbed his crotch all the way home, and he was looking forward to discovering what other treasures her tight jeans kept hidden. As he parked in her driveway and lowered the kickstand, he was suddenly aware of the sounds of a car engine at high speed rushing down the street. Jason grabbed Julie and pulled her to the ground behind his bike as he drew his .45 from his waistband. As the jilted soldier rolled past the house, he pulled his pistol with his left hand and emptied the magazine into the front of the house. Jason stayed crouched over Julie as the Toyota left the neighborhood. It was 2 a.m., but despite the hour, several porch lights came on at the sound of gunfire. Jason knew it would not be long before the cops were there. A drive-by shooting was not an everyday occurrence in this quiet neighborhood in Camden, Tennessee.

No bullets had come within ten feet of Jason and Julie, but there were several bricks along the front of the house with chunks missing. The damage was minimal, but Julie was freaking out. "Oh my God! Oh my God!" she kept screaming over and over. Jason continued to hold her for a few seconds until he was certain the danger had passed. He put his pistol away and stood up, bringing her with him. She was shaking and tears were flowing down her cheeks. She only wore minimal makeup, because she had a very natural beauty, but what little there was now ran in streaks down her cheeks. "Oh my

God!" she said again before adding, "What the fuck just happened?"

"Looks like your old boyfriend isn't too happy about getting dumped." The first police siren wailed through the early morning quiet. "The cops will be here in a minute. Are you going to be okay? They're going to have a lot of questions."

"Oh my God! I can't believe he would do this! What was he thinking?"

Jason took her by both shoulders and gently shook her. Looking directly into her eyes he said, "Listen dammit! Do you hear those sirens? The cops are coming, and you need to get control of yourself. Tell them about the bar, and let them know where that jackass lives. He won't be back here tonight, and he'll be in jail by tomorrow, so you don't have to worry about him anymore."

The first police car turned onto the street, and the siren was deafening. More bedroom and porch lights were coming on in the normally quiet neighborhood. A few people were out on their stoops wearing bathrobes and pajamas. As the car stopped at the end of Julie's driveway, Jason held her hand and led her down to the officer.

By the time the officers finished taking their statements, the soldier was under arrest. Armed with his name and address, the other officers had no trouble tracking him down. In fact, they arrived at his house as soon as he did, and they took his freshly-fired 9mm and its empty magazine as evidence. He was not going to be getting out of jail anytime soon.

Two days later, Jason walked back into the bar, and could instantly tell the atmosphere was different. The IRON KINGZ were much friendlier, and even bought an occasional beer for him. Lex came up to him during a lull in the action and said, "Rat vouched for you. We're going on an overnight ride to Cincinnati this weekend. If you want to come with us, you can. If you say yes, then when we get back we'll make you a Prospect. That's the most difficult step toward full membership. It's fucking hard, and you have to be totally committed. If you don't want to be a member, just say so now, and nobody will ever ask you again. You only get one shot, and this is it, so it's now or never."

Jason looked Lex in the eyes. His expression was hard and serious, but with a hint of sadness born of a lifetime of riding, fighting, and trying to stay on the razor's edge between legitimate businessman and outlaw biker. Jason had no friends who were not in this room. He had been shunned by the college he attended, the Marine Corps, the Highway Patrol, and the VA. This was the only place and the only group of people that he could actually be himself around and not get judged for his appearance or his past. He saw that the members of the club stood up for each other, and valued their brotherhood more than life itself. "Sounds good to me," he said.

"Okay then. We leave from here at 8:00 Saturday morning. Don't be late. "

And with that, his whole life changed.

Chapter 22

Saturday morning dawned with a cold rain. It was March, and this transitional month between winter and spring was still roaring like a lion. "This is gonna suck," Jason thought to himself as he put on his leathers. He knew that as a Hang-Around, he had to at least show up. If the ride was cancelled, nobody was going to call him, not that they could even if they wanted to, because his phone number changed every week when he purchased a new burn phone. No, he had to be there, because this was his only shot at becoming a member of the IRON KINGZ and that was his last chance at brotherhood.

It was less than a mile to the bar from his trailer, but the rain was coming down hard and Jason was drenched by the time he pulled into the parking lot at 7:50. A few other bikes were there, and their riders looked hung over and not excited about the prospect of traveling almost 400 miles in this weather. Lex and the Vice President, a burly no-nonsense personality named Dirty Ed pulled into the parking lot at exactly 8:00. All the members lined up behind them. The club's Road Captain, Stoner, went to the head of the line. His job was to plan the route and lead the ride. Everyone else fell into formation with Jason all the way at the back behind the Prospects. For now, he was at the bottom of the food chain, and he resolutely took his place at the end of the line.

The rain kept up all weekend, and the ride to and from Cincinnati was just as miserable as Jason had imagined. The party however, was very good. They were hosted by another outlaw club, the WARMONGERS. Their clubhouse was nice and was crowded with women, booze, drugs, and every manner of vice anyone could imagine. Jason quietly sipped Budweiser and stayed around the IRON KINGZ. Without a patch on his back, he had no genuine standing with either club, so he was there only under the good graces of the IRON KINGZ, and they were there only under the good graces of the WARMONGERS. The latter only tolerated him out of respect for their guests, but Jason knew he needed to walk a tight line.

The following week, Lex told Jason to be sure to be at Ape-Hangers on church night. Following the members-only meeting, the club members filed out into the bar and surrounded him. Lex spoke: "Listen. You did everything right on the run to Cincinnati, and tonight the club voted to make you a Prospect. I'll be your sponsor, which means I'm responsible to teach you how to be an IRON KING. Don't let it go to your fucking head. You're a long fucking way from being a patch, but I think you probably have what it takes. I've never sponsored a Prospect who didn't get patched in, and you ain't gonna be the first. If you have any doubts about this at all, you damn well better let us know right now before I put my neck on the line for you. Prospecting is serious business, and we're not gonna cut you any slack. You fuck up, and the whole fucking club will beat your ass." The expressions on all the members' faces let Jason know the truth of this statement.

Jason looked closely at Lex. The coldness in his eyes showed he was serious, and that if Jason did not take it seriously, he would never wear the IRON KINGZ patch. "Lex, I appreciate you telling me. If you sponsor me, I won't let you down. Every member of the IRON

KINGZ will have one hundred percent of my loyalty."

"Okay. Don't fuck this up." And with that, Lex handed Jason a black leather vest with only a bottom rocker on the back that read Prospect. "This is the last patch we'll sew on for you. IF, and I mean IF you earn another, it will be your job to get it on and get it on fast."

Donning the vest, Jason looked at the club and said, "Thanks. I won't let you down."

⸺◦《◦》◦⸺

Jason's status as a Prospect meant more of the IRON KINGZ spent time with him. Actually, it was Jason who had to spend time with them, because the purpose of prospecting was to see if you could fit into the club. The patched members viewed the rest of society as beneath them and unworthy of their respect. "Respect Few, Fear None" was emblazoned on a patch almost every 1%er wore on their vest, and most of them had it tattooed somewhere on their body. As a Prospect, Jason rated only a modicum of respect from patched members, but since he had actually been around them for several months and the ones who had not seen him fight the soldier and steal his girl had at least heard of it, he was treated better than the other Prospects most of the time.

The Sergeant at Arms for the club was a huge man named Bull. He stood over 6'6" tall and easily weighed 400 pounds. He was not fat, but was built more like a defensive end. At 34 years old, he had been a member for over 8 years, and had a patch that most of the others did not. A small pair of smoking pistols with their barrels crossed. Every patch that every member wore meant something, and

Jason suspected this one meant Bull had killed for the club. He had been charged with assault and other various minor felonies several times, and had once served 18 months in the state penitentiary. He was the club's enforcer, responsible for administering discipline and punishment as the club saw fit. Jason had seen him fight once, a few months earlier, when Ratchet got drunk and belligerent with the Club President. Bull lifted him up off his feet with one hand and threw him across a pool table. When Ratchet responded by picking up a pool cue and breaking it across Bull's head, he was met with a shrug as Bull unleashed a looping right cross that broke the biker's jaw and left him unconscious. A couple of other members took him to the hospital, and nothing was ever said again. Ratchet was back in Ape-Hangers a few days later with his jaw wired shut, and drinking Budweiser through a straw. He was much better behaved, however.

Bull approached Jason and asked "Why don't you have any tats? Every biker I know has tats."

"I guess I just gotta be different."

"Yeah. Different. I get that. We're all different. That's why we're here. This club, the IRON KINGZ, it ain't some group of motorcycle enthusiasts. Leave that to the AMA. We don't give a shit about anybody but us, and this is our business, not our hobby. It's our whole life. If you think you can get in without paying the price, you're kidding yourself and wasting our time. Nobody here has anything but the club, and every one of us will protect it with his life."

"I get it Bull. I got nothing else either. That's why I'm here. You guys are the only friends I've got."

"We're not your friends yet, Prospect. Serve your time, then talk about friends." Bull walked away, and Jason did not know what to make of the conversation. Bull could have just been testing him, or he could be serious. There was no way to know, because the patched members were only honest among themselves. Outsiders, even Hang Arounds and Prospects, were never trusted.

———————«()»———————

There were other runs Jason made with the club during the next couple of months. In May, they lived in tents for Bike Week in Myrtle Beach, South Carolina, one of four mandatory runs the club made every year. The other three were Daytona in February, before Jason was a Prospect; Laconia, New Hampshire in June, and Sturgis, South Dakota in August. As the club was readying for the Laconia run, Lex called Jason over to where he was standing with Dirty Ed and Bull. "It's a long way to Laconia; are you sure you're ready?" asked Lex.

Jason shot him a quizzical look and glanced at the other two men. No one was smiling. "Of course I'm ready," he said to Lex.

Lex smiled and said, "Get your ass to the end of the line, Prospect. The hell has only begun. You know the rules, and they are enforced at the end of a Patch's fist or with outright banishment from the club."

"I got it, Lex. I got your back."

"Let's hope so." Lex had already mounted his bike and cranked the engine before Jason could say anything else. He roared away with the rest of the club following. Jason hustled back to his bike and raced out of the parking lot so as not to be left behind. Less than a mile from Ape-Hanger's, the whole club was running wheel-to-wheel at 80 miles per hour. Jason's Road Glide easily kept pace.

Their first stop was along some two-lane highway in Kentucky. The small picnic area was unoccupied, and Jason was confused why they stopped there. Typically, they stopped at gas stations, bars, and fast food joints. After the bikes were parked, all the members formed a semi-circle around Dirty Ed and Lex. Jason and the other two Prospects waited on the rear outskirts of the group. Dirty Ed spoke, "Our sister club from Bowling Green is going to meet us here in about 30 minutes. Everybody chill out and make sure your bikes are running right. I don't want to have to stop to fix something that can be fixed now."

As the group dispersed back to their bikes, a couple of them lit up a joint and started passing it around. Jason always passed on the dope. He told them his first love was booze and that was all he wanted. He was retightening the bedroll on his bike when Bull yelled out, "Hey Prospect!" Jason turned and walked toward him. "I need you to carry this for me," Bull said as he handed Jason a .38 caliber Smith and Wesson snub-nosed revolver. Jason never left home without his own .45 automatic, but now as a full-fledged Prospect, it was his job to help the members in any way they asked. Bull had felony convictions, and it was illegal for him to be armed. Prospects routinely carried contraband for the members, and since Jason had no convictions, he could possess as many weapons as he wanted.

Their club's brothers from Bowling Green arrived right on time, and after a few handshakes and hugs, the whole group took off on the road together. Now 30 bikes strong, they were a formidable obstacle heading north to Laconia. They rode hard and camped in Indiana that night. The party was loud and lasted well into the night. The families who were also camping there probably did not get much sleep.

The next day they were in southern New York and were joined by their brothers from the only chapter in Delaware. Rat was a member of this group, and he and Jason enjoyed their brief reunion. Rat made it a point to only screw with the other Prospects, never Jason. "You'll get enough shit from the other Patches" he said. "I'm not gonna coddle you, but I'll find other Prospects to fuck with." Rat was on a brand-new Screaming Eagle Softail. Jason thought to himself, "How could he ever afford that?" but let the thought drop. How a brother earned his money was not club business.

The party in Laconia was tremendous. As a Prospect, Jason did not get to enjoy the full extent of the festivities, because he spent most of the time watching over the club members' motorcycles while they partied in one bar or another. He met the IRON KINGZ National President at the rally. His name was Goat, and he looked Hispanic. At least 60 years old, his ponytail was mottled with many gray hairs. His face was weather-beaten, and although he only stood about 5'8", his demeanor showed he was in charge and not to be trifled with. His chapter was in Melbourne, Florida, about 100 miles south of Daytona. There was another chapter in Orlando. For Bike Week in Laconia, the IRON KINGZ rented several cabins in a remote campground on the shores of a lake. One night Goat called a meeting in his cabin for all the club officers from all the chapters. Jason counted several different territory rockers walking into the closed-door meeting while he and some other members who were not officers stood outside drinking beer.

"Wonder what's going on in there?" one with a Delaware patch asked another with an Alabama patch.

"Fuck if I know. It's officer shit." Then, "Hey Prospects! Get some more beer over here!"

Jason and another Prospect hustled down toward a cabin with at least 20 coolers sitting in front of it. The official "Bar Cabin" was kept well stocked during Bike Week. They brought an entire cooler of beer back and sat it on the ground in front of the members. "Now get the fuck out of here!" was their only thanks.

————))((————

Over the next several days, rumors swirled around the details of the meeting. Information slowly leaked out. Rival gangs in the area were pressuring the Delaware chapter, making it difficult for them to operate both their legitimate and illegitimate businesses. As the smallest and most isolated IRON KINGZ chapter, they were struggling to maintain their territory. A war with the other gangs was inevitable, but there was no way to win it from their current position. Goat's plan was two-fold. First, he would disband the Delaware Chapter and have the members absorbed into the Southern Chapters. Second, they would amass the tools of war and return to Delaware to retake it by force.

Ray was joining Jason's chapter, and that suited both men just fine. Jason knew that the club would need money and weapons in order to fight, and he was certain he could help on at least one of those fronts. He despised war, but if his brothers were going to fight, he was not about to abandon them. He knew Ray had experienced a lot of trouble during his time in the Marines, but he also knew the heart that all Marines have. They would never let their brothers down, and they understood how to fight.

The night before Laconia ended, Jason saw Lex sitting on the front porch of his cabin alone. Approaching the steps, he said "Hey Lex. Got a minute? I have an idea I want to run by you."

"Sure Prospect. What's up?"

"I know it's not my place to tell the club what they need to do, but before we all go to Delaware and start throwing our weight around, there's a few things we're gonna need. First, we're gonna need weapons, and I'm not convinced pistols and sawed-off shotguns will be enough. Even if every member of the IRON KINGZ shows up for the fight, we're still likely to be outnumbered and outgunned. The guys we're up against won't respect us unless we scare the shit out of them, and show them we're the baddest motherfuckers on the block."

"So what do you suggest?"

"Well, if we just go up there and start shooting, it will be a losing situation for everybody. Even if we don't get killed, we're all likely to end up in prison, and then we won't be able to do anything. I think if the other clubs see some serious firepower from us, we can likely run them off without having to wage all-out war."

"What kind of firepower are you talking about? Fucking machine guns ain't exactly readily available."

"What if they were? What if I told you I could get fully automatic, totally untraceable AKs by the dozen?"

"I'm listening."

"Just leave it up to me. I can get as many as you want, and I can get them quick."

"Listen Prospect. I'm not in the habit of just trusting guys to get things done. You're gonna have to show me something."

"Give me two weeks, and I can have AKs in the clubhouse. I'll show you all you need. We can have them before the Sturgis run."

"I'll be watching, Prospect. Don't fuck this up. You get the AKs and I'll talk to the officers about what to do with them." With that, Lex rose from his seat, and walked inside the cabin. Jason sat alone on the porch. It was getting late, and the whole IRON KINGZ nation had a long ride in the morning. He cracked open a beer and contemplated brotherhood.

Was it worth the cost? Could he leave it behind and not look back? There were no easy answers, but a man alone in the world was just that: a lonely man.

Jason needed to be part of something bigger than himself. He needed to belong somewhere, to something. The world had rejected him, and these men, despite their faults were his last chance at belonging.

After an hour, he shuffled off to the cabin where he was staying with the other Prospects and slept.

The morning dawned bright and clear. The sky was as blue as Jason had ever seen it. The entire IRON KINGZ nation mounted their bikes and roared away from Laconia. Jason and the other Prospects brought up the rear of the pack and marveled at the nearly 200 members stretched out before them on the highway. There was a real sense of power and belonging. The miles floated away beneath the tires of his Road Glide, and the engine thumped away rhythmically underneath his seat.

Were it not for the difficult task he faced during the upcoming month, he would have been at total peace. Getting additional shipments of AKs from Kuwait was no problem. Muhammed could ship as many as he wanted, but getting them back to Tennessee was going to require some serious planning. To this point, Jason had never seen a single AK he imported. They were picked up at the Atlanta Cargo Terminal while he and the Familia members waited on a hilltop outside of town.

Using a burn phone when the IRON KINGZ stopped for the night, he called Muhammed and asked him to double the shipments for the next month. After destroying the phone, he used a new one to call Julio.

"Hola," Julio answered on the other end of the line.

"Hey," Jason replied. "It's me. I have a deal for you, but I need a favor in return."

"Like what?" Julio did not seem to be in a good mood. This was dangerous, and he knew it.

"Instead of your uncle importing spices just once next month, he needs to import them three times. I'll take half the spices for my own restaurant, and you can have your regular shipments for free. I just need your guys to deliver my spices to me."

Julio was silent for a moment. "That's a lot of risk. We can do it, but I want two months of free spices in return."

Jason could feel his anger rising. The plan he proposed would cost him $7000. Julio's offer would bankrupt him entirely. He was not in a mood to negotiate. "Listen motherfucker. I'm not dicking around with you. I've made you a lot of money, and you have your street cred back because of what I've given you. If you ever want to see another spice, you will do this the way I tell you. I can sell to your competition as easy as I can to you. What's it gonna look like down there then? You won't be the honcho on the block anymore. Your ass will be right back where you started. Now do we have a deal or not?"

There was another long silence. "Si. We have a deal."

"Good. Now here's how to get the spices to me."

Chapter 23

The party around the campfire that night was just as crazy as the ones in Laconia. While the bikers smoked joints and drank beer, Jason slipped away from the pack, laid his bedroll in the shadow of his bike and tried to get some sleep. He no more than dozed off when Bull came by and kicked him awake. "Hey Prospect! Get your pansy ass up. You don't sleep till the Patches sleep. Now go out in the woods and get some more dead limbs and shit for the fire. We're running out."

Jason rose wearily. He and the other Prospects had gathered enough wood for two nights when the IRON KINGZ first pulled into the campground, and he knew Bull was just proving a point. Prospects were slaves to the Patches, and he was exercising his authority. Such was the price of membership.

Pulling on his boots, Jason staggered aimlessly through the campground looking for firewood. Outside the confines of the IRON KINGZ' area, the families who thought they were enjoying a nice summer camping trip were trying to get some rest. It was after midnight, and most of the lights in the campers and RVs were off. As Jason surveyed the scene, he noticed smoldering embers in a fire pit next to a pop-up camper. No one was around, and there were several oak logs next to the pit. "Fuck it," he thought. "They can spare a couple of these, and it'll get Bull off my ass for the night. He probably doesn't even remember he told me to do this."

He grabbed an armful of split oak firewood and started up the hill towards the IRON KINGZ' area. A dog inside a nearby motorhome started barking, and two lights came on. The first was inside and the other was over the door on the outside. Jason ducked behind a pickup truck as the door came open. An older man wearing pajama shorts and a white undershirt stood in the entrance. He was only about ten yards away, but he could not see Jason peering through the truck window in the dark. "What is it, George?" a woman's voice behind the man asked.

"Nothing I guess. I don't see anything."

"Those bikers are still up there," the woman said.

"Yeah. I'm going to complain tomorrow to the owners. They've ruined our whole night. It's like they don't even care that there are good families here, and nobody can sleep around those damn bikes and all the noise they make. I'm going to tell the owners they won't be seeing us here ever again if that's the kind of people they let in here."

"You should call the cops. They're disturbing the peace."

"I don't want to cause any more trouble than I have to."

"If you don't call them, I will. I am NOT going to have my vacation ruined by a bunch of criminals with absolutely no regard for anybody but themselves."

"Oh, to hell with it. I'll call them." He closed the door and walked back inside.

Jason hurried up the hill and found Lex. "Hey man, I just heard somebody down the hill say they were calling the cops on us. You might want to start stashing things in case they decide to search when they get here."

"No shit? Fuck those motherfuckers," Lex said. He was high, and Jason knew this was not going to end well for the IRON KINGZ if the cops found them all sitting around with drugs and guns in plain sight.

"Listen Lex. Unless you want to bail out about half the nation in the morning, you need to get the guys to hide their shit."

Lex did not answer; he just staggered away and sat down by the fire. He pulled a joint from behind his ear, and lit it with a stick from the edge of the fire. As he passed it around, Jason walked up and said to the crowd around the fire, "Listen up. The cops are going to be here in about five minutes. They're going to talk to everybody. Maybe run warrant checks. Even if they don't, all they have to see is you guys burning a joint around the fire, and they'll have cause to search. What do you think will happen then? You need to get your shit together unless you want to wake up in jail." It was a rare thing for a Prospect to speak to a Patch like this, and to speak to a nearly fifty Patches at once was suicidal. A normal reaction would have been for all of them to bull-rush the belligerent Prospect and beat him down, but instead there was stunned silence.

As the light of recognition began to dawn in a few eyes, they began to stir and move off toward their sites. Others were awakened, hushed whispers were heard, and the sound of saddlebags being opened, and things being flung into the woods resonated throughout the area. Within ten minutes, the entire site was clean as a whistle.

As the cleanup was ending, two patrol vehicles entered the campground winding their way through the sites towards the IRON KINGZ' area. When they approached, only about a dozen members were left around the fire. Except for Lex, they were all sober, and Jason was among them. The first deputy exited his car and walked toward the group. "What's going on guys?"

"Not much, how about you?" one of the patches replied. His name was Weird Eddie and he was the Treasurer of the Kentucky Chapter.

"Got a call about some noise up this way."

"Well," Weird Eddie answered, "that may have been the case a while back, but as you can see, it's pretty quiet now."

"Uh huh," grunted the deputy in reply.

The second deputy had joined him now. "You guys been drinking?" he asked.

"Sure, we've had a few. Getting ready to go to bed now, though."

Both deputies were shining their lights around the various campsites now occupied by peaceful, sleeping bikers. "You guys don't have anything illegal in here do you?" the second deputy asked as he continued to scan the area with his light.

"No deputy we don't," came the answer from one of the other patched members.

"Then ya'll won't mind if we look around, will you?" the deputy said.

"Actually, we would mind that very much," Jason said, stepping forward. We've got a long ride tomorrow, and our guys are trying to get some rest. There's no noise up here now, and there won't be any more tonight. There's nothing for you to see here, and nobody's going to consent to any searches."

This caught both deputies off guard. They stared at Jason, and the second deputy spoke again. "I need to see your ID."

"Why? I've done nothing wrong and you ain't got no reason to see it."

"Listen smartass, I can have a dozen cars here in twenty minutes. We will search every inch of this area, and we will charge everybody here with public drunkenness and disturbing the peace. And that's just for starters. Once we find dope and guns, that ups it all to felonies, and then we'll run warrant checks on your entire crew. My guess is a bunch of those will come back as WANTED in a bunch of different states. So once you're done serving your felony time here, you can go to the next state and start the process all over again."

He continued: "Your other option is to cooperate now, and maybe I can go easy on you and your friends. The choice is yours. The easy way or the hard way. Now what's it gonna be?"

Jason stood his ground. He knew the law better than either of these guys, and he knew this small-time department in middle of nowhere probably did not have a dozen cars on the entire force. He figured these two guys were probably the only two on duty in the entire county, and there was no way they were going to waste their entire night rousting a bunch of bikers who were leaving in the morning. "Call 'em in," he said. "We still won't consent to any search."

The deputies huddled together and spoke in hushed tones for several minutes. The bikers stood around the fire and watched. Lex was there, and he was looking at Jason very closely. Jason saw what he thought looked like a new attitude in Lex's eyes: Respect.

When the deputies again turned toward the bikers, the first one spoke. "We're going to be near this area all night. I don't even need anyone to complain again. If I hear anything louder than a mouse fart from this campground, I'll arrest everyone here for disturbing the peace. In either case, I'll be back here in the morning, and there better not be so much as a trace of you guys. Pack your shit and hit the road early."

Jason could see the anger rising in Lex. He was not in the habit of taking any lip from the law, and he did not intend to start tonight. Knowing any challenge to the deputies at this point would only invite trouble, Jason was quick to step forward and speak. "We got it, deputy. All you're asking is that we do what we're gonna do anyway." He gave a quick glance over his shoulder at Lex to make sure he had stopped. "You won't hear anything out of this camp tonight, and we're outta here in the morning. Y'all have a good night." He turned back toward Lex and said, "Hey Prez, these guys were just leaving. How about I get you a cold one and then we'll hit the sack?"

"Get us all a beer, and we'll watch these guys drive off."

Jason turned back to the deputies, and there was a momentary stare down before they began walking back to their cars. Breathing a sigh of relief to himself, he walked over to the nearest cooler and retrieved several beers for the bikers. Lex was the first to speak. "Prospect, you handled that pretty well."

And that was about as close as any Prospect would ever come to getting a "thank you" from a patched member. Without even finishing his beer, Jason grunted an acknowledgement to Lex and walked back toward his bike. He was tired and ready for some sleep.

Chapter 24

Back in Paris, during the next church meeting the Club voted to change Jason's PROSPECT patch to a TENNESSEE patch. He knew it was because he saved their asses during the trip back from Laconia. He was one step closer to being part of his final brotherhood.

The following week, Jason returned to Atlanta. This was his first delivery of AKs for the club, and he traveled in his Jeep so he could haul them back. He had rented a storage unit in a large complex and paid cash for six months up front. Julio and company had stashed the weapons inside it the day before. Working the combination on the lock, Jason raised the metal door and saw a steel air cargo box sitting in the middle of the floor. He had not known exactly how Muhammed and his cousin packaged the shipments, and this was the first time he laid eyes on anything he had imported.

Opening the box, he saw several wooden compartments containing a variety of spices. The smell was very pungent, but the spices were just a cover and were not high quality. The stench of cheap peppers, garlic, and curry mixed with the sweetness of cinnamon, thyme, and rosemary. Jason turned his head aside to lessen the effect on his senses. Removing the wooden racks and setting them aside, he looked back at ten perfectly clean AK-47s. They showed the wear and tear of use on the battlefields of Iraq, but these were some of the toughest weapons ever manufactured and Jason knew that every one of them would work flawlessly when the trigger was pulled.

He quickly put everything back in its place and sealed the steel shipping container. There would be plenty of time to admire his weapons once he was back in Paris. The box was heavy, and the handles were not set up for one man to lift it by himself. Nonetheless, Jason grabbed it by one end, hefted it into his Jeep, then shoved it all the way in from the rear. Closing the tailgate, he exited the storage unit and locked it behind him. He needed to get back to Ape-Hangers and talk to Lex about what the IRON KINGZ needed to do.

⎯⎯⎯⎯━◉◉◉━⎯⎯⎯⎯

It was late when he drove into town, and Ape-Hangers was closed. Jason went straight to his trailer and got some much-needed rest. The following morning, he was knocking on Lex's door before 8:00 a.m. When the sleepy president opened the door he barked, "What the fuck, Prospect? What do you want so fucking early?"

"I got the AKs in my Jeep."

"No shit?" Lex grunted and said, "Drive it around back and we'll bring them through the back of the garage."

Jason did as he was told, and when the men were looking at the weapons, Lex marveled, "You actually did it. I'll be damned. These are the first AKs I've seen since I left Vietnam in '69. Haven't changed much."

"This is just the first ten. I'll have another ten in two weeks. After that, we can lay our plans for Delaware."

"Yeah, about that. Goat wants to handle Delaware after the Sturgis run. We'll be back from that in the middle of August, then we can go take care of business. We have a couple of girls that the guys used to bang keeping an eye on the competition there. They already gave us a lead on where the clubhouses are located, and we should know how many members there are soon."

"That's good," Jason replied. "The more info we can get, the better off we'll all be. It makes sense to plan this thing as detailed as possible, otherwise we might get our asses handed to us."

Lex looked angry at the insinuation that any number of other gangsters might be able to hurt a single IRON KING, no matter the odds. He barked at Jason, "Just get the fucking guns and leave the planning to the people who know what the hell they're doing."

"That's my point, Lex. I'm not convinced that most of our guys are really ready for a turf war. If we don't do this smart, we're gonna wind up dead or in jail."

"Fucking Prospect," Lex was yelling into Jason's face. The stench of last night's beer was heavy on his breath, but Jason met his stare eye-to-eye. "Have you ever been in a war against another gang?"

"No, but I've been in a war in Iraq, and I think that might count for something," Jason growled back at his sponsor and his president.

"You don't know shit, Prospect. I've been in Vietnam, and that was one thing. A street war with another gang is a different story. It takes evil and experience to win it, and that's exactly what we're gonna do. Bring evil and experience to Delaware, and claim that shit as ours. The IRON KINGZ have never lost an inch of territory to another gang and these motherfuckers in Delaware are gonna wish they'd never seen our patch. We're gonna send those motherfuckers home or to hell, and I don't care which!"

Jason decided not to respond. He just said, "Okay Lex. Y'all are the bosses. I'll have the other ten AKs here in two weeks, then we can go to Sturgis."

Chapter 25

The Tennessee Chapter of the IRON KINGZ MC gathered in front of Ape-Hangers early in the morning on the first day of August. It promised to be a hot ride to Sturgis, and the trip was the longest one the club took every year. It was over 1,300 miles one way, and the club would be gone for nearly three weeks. Sturgis was the best party of the year, and everybody was eager to get there. Bikers had their Ol' Ladies with them, and bedrolls, tents, and bags of clothing were strapped all over the bikes. Jason sometimes brought Julie along on rides with the club, but never on long trips. As a Prospect, he was too busy playing slave to the members to spare time for a woman.

The club's newly-elected Road Captain, the least desirable officer's spot in the club, was a 30-year old man named Baldy. He had been in the IRON KINGZ for over three years, and he was unemployed. His nickname clearly came from his premature baldness, but he made up for it with a Fu-Man-Chu mustache, the ends of which hung at least six inches below his chin. His motorcycle was among the saddest of the lot. It was an old Shovelhead with a kickstart that was left over from when Harley Davidson was owned by AMC in the 1970s. It leaked so much oil Baldy had to add more at virtually every fuel stop. Breakdowns on his bike were common, and usually resulted in somebody having to stay behind and help him fix it when it stranded him on the side of the road. He swore it was in great shape for the Sturgis run, but Jason had his doubts.

As the club rolled toward Sturgis, Jason enjoyed the day. It was nearly 100 degrees, but the cloudless sky and green of the trees and fields soothed him. He never minded riding in hot weather, and since there were about twenty bikes in this group, they hardly stopped at intersections in the small towns they rode through even when the traffic lights were red. A couple of the members would use their bikes to block the cross-streets while the group passed. The cops never messed with them as long as they kept riding and got out of their jurisdiction. No cop from Podunk, USA was interested in tangling with a large group of bikers, so the club never really slowed down except when they stopped for gas.

They were crossing the state of Missouri when Jason realized Baldy had one major shortcoming as a Road Captain. He could not read a map. "They should have called him a 'Road Lieutenant'," Jason chuckled to himself, remembering a truism from the Corps that Lieutenants were known for being unable to read maps. It seemed as if Baldy was navigating by the sun, but had no idea that it rose in the east, set in the west, and west was the direction they needed to be traveling. They twisted and turned their way through some town in the middle of nowhere and emerged heading east. After another hundred miles of travel, they finally stopped for gas. Jason went straight to Baldy at the pump. "Hey man, do you realize we're riding east? We should be in Kansas City tonight, but it looks more like we'll be in St. Louis."

"Fuck you Prospect. I know what I'm doing."

"Have you looked at a map?"

"I said fuck you. Now get away from me."

"Hey dude, I'm just trying to help." Jason turned and walked back to the pump to finish gassing up his own bike. He saw Baldy talking to Lex and then both of them went inside the gas station and pulled a state map off the rack. Lex looked frustrated, and Baldy looked apologetic, but when the club got back on the road, they were westbound.

Baldy eventually got the club to Sturgis, but Jason's odometer told him they rode almost 500 extra miles getting there because they spent as much time lost as they did going in the right direction. Under normal circumstances, Baldy would have been fired, fined, and bruised by the club for these transgressions, but since he was Lex's son, he was protected. Nobody wanted to mess with the son of the president.

— ((0)) —

The party at Sturgis was one for the ages. Everywhere they went was a sea of motorcycles, beer, and half-dressed women. The Knuckle Saloon downtown was where they spent the majority of their days. It had a boxing ring set up in the middle of an open courtyard surrounded on all four sides with two stories of open viewing. Guys who thought they were tough could sign up to fight and would be matched with someone else roughly their same weight. The fights were timed and refereed according to UFC rules, and if neither fighter quit or was knocked out after three rounds the winner was declared by the loudest cheers from the crowds.

As they were watching two middleweights slug it out one

afternoon, Lex said to Jason, "You should sign up to fight somebody."

"No thanks, Lex. I don't do that for fun."

"How about for money? We can match you up against a guy from some other club, and take side bets. You win, and you can take half the profit."

"Not interested."

"I'm not really asking, Prospect. There's a club here called the DESERT BASTARDS. Their guy is undefeated in this ring in the last three years. They'll match him up against anybody, but you can take him. I've seen you fight, and you're the only one I know who can beat him. The BASTARDS have won so much money off this guy that they actually give 2-to-1 or 3-to-1 odds. We can easily make three or four thousand dollars off this. All you gotta do is get in there and whoop his ass."

"So you're telling me that if I beat this guy I get $2000? Okay. I'm in because I'm broke. Not because I like to fight." And with that, Jason signed his name to the waiver. Within minutes, he was shirtless and bootless in the ring. The MMA gloves they gave him were still sweaty inside from the last guy who wore them.

When his opponent Big Bo emerged from the crowd, Jason knew he had a hard day's work in front of him. Big Bo was at least 6' 8" and weighed over 500 pounds. "Fuck you, Lex," he thought to himself. "What the fuck have you gotten me into?" His world turned red as his anger at the situation rose.

The crowd had seen Big Bo pummel so many opponents that the outcome was a foregone conclusion in their minds. The cheers for him were enormous while most of them looked at Jason as if he was a lamb led to the slaughter.

When they met in the center of the ring, Bo looked down at Jason with an expression that was fierce and fearless. Jason met his eyes, and never blinked. They touched gloves and got ready to battle. The bell for round one rang and Jason charged across the ring before Bo could even step from his corner. The speed of the charge caught both Bo and the crowd off guard. He held his arms in front of his face to weather this initial assault, but rather than punch, Jason flung his right knee into Bo's immense gut.

The air came out of Bo's lungs in a rush, but he stepped to the side and threw jab that missed, followed by a sweeping right hook that Jason ducked. The wind from the punch over Jason's head told him that if it had landed, he might well be unconscious on the ring floor right now. He backed up and took a traditional fighting pose.

Bo lunged again with a straight left that Jason sidestepped. With Bo off-balance and his left side toward Jason, Jason threw a hard left uppercut into his ribcage and a looping overhand right that landed directly on Bo's left ear. Before he could back away, Jason kicked him behind his left knee and brought him to the ground.

With Bo flat on his back, Jason crouched and flung another knee into the side of his head. Dazed, Bo tried to cover up, but Jason's speed and aggressiveness prevented it. Jason was on top of his opponent now, raining punch after punch into the man's face. Within seconds, the referee was pulling him back, and Bo was nearly unconscious, bleeding onto the mat. He rose slowly to his feet, while the crowd threw dollar bills into the ring for Jason. He left them there and walked out to get dressed and find Lex.

Lex found him first as he emerged from the dressing room and yelled, "That was beautiful man! I've never seen anything like it! The DESERT BASTARDS want a rematch." As he said this, he pressed $500 into Jason's hand.

"What's this?"

"That's your money."

"You said thousands. This is hundreds."

"I had to spread it around to some of the other guys."

"What? Fuck you. I ain't getting back in that ring for you. I coulda been killed, and all I get is five hundred?"

Lex looked unhappy and handed another hundred to Jason. "That's all there is until you fight again."

"What are you, my manager? I didn't want to fight in the first place, and then I get ripped off for fifteen hundred bucks, and now you want me to do it all over again? Nobody's gonna give you odds now, so my next take would probably be less than a hundred. I ain't doing it, Lex. If you want more money, you go fight yourself or get somebody else to do it for you. I'm your Prospect, not your bitch." Without waiting for a reply, Jason turned on his heel and walked through the crowd to find a beer.

—※—

On Wednesday of Sturgis Bike Week, there was a parallel

celebration about one hundred miles away in Hulett, Wyoming. Ham and Jam No Panties Wednesday had been going on for years, and always attracted a big crowd. Naturally, Baldy got the club lost on the ride there. Eventually, they parked their bikes on the edge of town and enjoyed the sights in an Old West town that still had hitching posts in front of the buildings. The posts were not just for show, either. It was clear that any other time of year; horses were a legitimate source of transportation in these parts, but during Bike Week, the local cowboys stayed on their ranches.

Vendor booths lined the streets, selling everything from custom leather to cold beer. It was early afternoon and the club stayed together as they walked the streets. Every corner had two police officers standing on it to prevent any trouble, and they cast a wary eye towards the IRON KINGZ whenever the club walked past. There probably was not a police officer in Hulett any other time of year, but during Bike Week, the Wyoming Highway Patrol along with deputies from around the state joined forces to keep the peace.

Baldy ducked into a small alleyway and Jason saw him snorting a line of meth. Ever the good Prospect, Jason remained at the entrance to the alley to block anyone's view and give Baldy some cover. Walking ahead with the rest of the club, Lex looked back over his shoulder and nodded to Jason. He knew Lex appreciated the protection he provided, especially for his son.

Emerging from the alley, Baldy wiped his nose and said, "I need a cold beer, a shot of whiskey and some pussy." He patted Jason on the arm as he said this and smiled as if there was nothing else in the world to do.

"Let's catch up with the Brothers, and see about getting into a bar," Jason offered helpfully.

"No, fuck that," retorted Baldy. "Those motherfuckers will walk around half the day sipping beer and not even getting drunk. I came here to party, and if their old asses want to window-shop, that's their problem. I'm still young enough to get it up, and I'm ready to get drunk and get laid. You're the Prospect, and you're coming with me. I'll teach you how a real One Percenter parties."

Jason was disgusted by being stuck as Baldy's babysitter, and he knew it was not a good idea to go bar hopping in Hulett with a meth-head, but as the club was reaching the far end of the street and turning out of sight, Baldy led Jason into an Old West saloon complete with swinging doors. Inside, it was well-lit and authentic down to the last detail. A player piano stood in a corner. The bar where many a cowboy had sat was clearly over one hundred years old, and constructed from heavy walnut.

There were still empty seats at the small round tables on the floor because the real party would not kick off until well after sundown. A waitress no older than 20, wearing a string bikini and high heels approached the men as they sat down. "What can I get for you gentlemen?" she asked as she smiled and brushed back her long wavy brown hair.

Jason thought to himself that she probably traveled up from the University of Wyoming in Laramie just for this week, and might even pay for her school from the tips bikers handed out here. His thoughts were interrupted as Baldy placed his order. "Right now I'll have a bottle of Bud, and a shot of Jack. Later I'll have some of this." As he finished his sentence, he slapped her hard on her bare ass cheek. In an amazing display of composure, she stepped out of arm's reach from Baldy and looked at Jason. There was fear and anger in her eyes, and Jason tried to be reassuring with his own expression, as if to say, "It'll be all right. I'll get him under control."

"I'll just have a bottle of Bud," he said, and felt like his reassuring look did not get through. The girl walked away and he could clearly see a red handprint where Baldy had slapped her. He returned his attention to Baldy who was admiring his handiwork as he watched her move toward the bar. "Hey man. You gotta get it under control. It's not even dark yet. The cops got nothing better to do right now than lock you up."

Baldy's face flushed red and his anger and voice rose when he spoke. "Fuck you Prospect! You want to party like a One Percenter or not? Are you in or out?"

Jason could see some of the bikers in the bar looking their way, and he leaned across the table toward Baldy. Speaking in a hushed tone, he said, "Hey man, I'm in and you know it. But what I'm not in is jail. I'm trying to keep you out of it too. Now just slow down and enjoy your beer. There'll be plenty of time for all that other shit later."

The waitress returned with their drinks, but served from Jason's side of the table. He handed her a $20 bill and told her to keep the change, hoping that might calm things down. Baldy would have none of it. "Hey honey. Come over here and sit on my lap!"

She replied, "No thanks," with a disgusted look.

"Okay then, how about my face?" he stuck his tongue out and wiggled it at her. She backed away and walked to a dark corner where Jason saw her talking to someone in the shadows. Baldy downed his shot and chased it with half his bottle of Budweiser. Jason took a reserved sip from his beer.

From the shadows in the back of the bar, three large men emerged. They were wearing 1%er patches of their own, and they were hired security this week. They did not approach the table directly. Instead, they spread out on three sides of it leaving the door as the only escape route. "Give your enemy an avenue to flee," thought Jason, "for if he has no escape, his only option is to fight." The quote was from Sun Tzu, an ancient Chinese warrior and author of The Art of War. It was required reading for all Marines.

The men kept their distance, close enough to pounce, but far enough to not be obvious. Baldy, who was busy draining the remainder of his beer in one long gulp, was completely unaware. Jason took another tiny sip from his Budweiser, and thought about his options if the men decided to physically evict them. Baldy turned around and stood up. Holding the empty bottle over his head, he yelled, "Hey bitch! How about some more service over here?"

The men started moving in, and Jason jumped to his feet. "It's okay guys. It's okay. I've got him."

They stopped, and Baldy finally realized what was happening. Screaming at the top of his lungs, "Fuck you! I'm a fucking paying customer and I want some service!" Jason quickly stepped between him and the men, still waving them back and ushering Baldy toward the door.

"Come on man. Let's go."

"Fuck you Prospect! These motherfuckers ain't got shit on us. We're IRON KINGZ! Fuck them!"

Before Jason could get him to the door, two uniformed deputies, alerted by the all the commotion, walked in. Seeing them, Jason said,

"I've got him deputy. I'll get him out."

The deputies stepped aside to let Jason get the still struggling Baldy to the door just as Lex and the rest of the club walked in. "What the fuck?" said Lex.

A deputy, seeing the same patches on so many bikers, spoke to Lex. "Don't just get him out of the bar. Get him out of town. If I see him back here today, I will put his dumb ass in jail."

Out on the sidewalk now, Lex grabbed Baldy by the collar. "You could fuck up a wet dream!" Turning to Jason he said, "Get him back to Sturgis. We'll see you there tomorrow." Realizing he was not going to win this one, Baldy calmed down. He and Jason began the long walk back to the bikes while Lex and the rest of the club turned back toward the action in town.

Reaching the bikes, Baldy pulled out his meth bag and snorted some more right in plain view of anyone on the street. Jason looked around nervously, but no cops seemed to notice. Mounting his bike, Baldy said, "I'm still the Patch and you're still the Prospect. Don't forget that. I'm leading." He kicked the Shovelhead to life and roared down the street before Jason even turned the ignition on his own bike. Still, Baldy's old Shovelhead was no match for Jason's modern Road Glide, and he caught up by the time they reached the city limits. Baldy gunned the throttle on the open highway, and soon they were traveling at nearly 100 miles per hour.

Turning down a side road, Baldy never let off the throttle. This road was paved, but unmarked and narrow. It was in poor repair, and Jason was certain Baldy's bike was going to rattle apart and crash them both. A 1%er rule is that you stay close to the guys you are riding with, so Jason remained within a few feet of Baldy's rear tire, even at 90 miles per hour on a poor road that soon turned to gravel. Cresting a hill, Baldy's engine suddenly quit. Jason slowed quickly to avoid hitting the other man's bike as they coasted to a stop at the bottom.

They dismounted and the problem was easy to spot. Both of Baldy's spark plug wires were so old, they were held together only with electrical tape. One of them had broken again. He was pulling the roll of tape out of his saddlebag before Jason even walked over to see what was going on. "Do you even know where we are?" he asked.

"Yeah, it's not exactly like I remember it but this road comes out near the South Dakota border."

"Really?" Jason asked, incredulous. "It seems pretty desolate out here."

"Listen Prospect. I told you I know where we are. Now shut up and start stripping the tape off that wire. I've got to get this fucker put back together."

Jason went about his duty. They had not seen another vehicle, house, barn, or any other signs of life in at least thirty miles. For all he knew, this road would dead-end at some distant canyon. He doubted Baldy had any clue where they were either. His thoughts were interrupted by the unmistakable sounds of Harley-Davidson motorcycles approaching from behind them on the other side of the hill. He and Baldy both stopped what they were doing and turned to look in the direction of the noise. Jason thought to himself, "What other fools are as lost as us?" His answer came in an instant when four bikes ridden by BANDALEROS, another 1%er Club with all their chapters in the West, topped the hill and began slowing as they approached the stranded IRON KINGZ.

Jason stepped behind his bike and stood on the shoulder of the road as the BANDALEROS rolled to a stop. Behind him was a very tall and steep hillside, covered in rocks and sagebrush. It would have been a difficult climb anytime, but as a means of escape from this, it was no option at all. The four bikes parked in a semi-circle around the two men, and their riders got off. Jason noticed immediately that their bottom territory rockers read WYOMING. All four were large and powerful men. They wore black bandanas pulled low over their eyes, typical of Latino gangsters, and reminding Jason of the North Street Familia. All had tattoos that clearly came from a needle in a prison cell.

As the BANDALEROS walked up, one of them spoke. "IRON KINGZ with Tennessee rockers in Wyoming. I don't remember you asking permission to be here."

"We don't need permission," retorted Baldy. "It's Bike Week and that's a blanket exemption."

"It's Bike Week in South Dakota. Not here. Since you don't have permission, you're gonna need to pay the tax. I think $500 should cover it long enough for you to get out of the state."

"Look fucker. We're not alone, and we ain't paying no tax."

"You look alone to me," said the BANDALERO leader as the other three laughed. "Now let's talk about that tax." As he said this, one of the men untied an ax handle from his luggage rack and another pulled a large hunting knife from its sheath. "Now are you gonna pay willingly, or will we be taking our tax out in blood?"

As he finished saying this, Jason saw the third man pulling a revolver from his waistband. The world went red. In a flash, he pulled his own Colt .45 automatic and fired a round into the gunman's chest. He fired again hitting the knife-wielding BANDALERO. The man with the ax handle was nearest Jason and drew it back like a major leaguer swinging for the fences. From a distance of less than three feet, Jason shot him twice, once in the chest and then in the face. This all took place in only a few seconds, and Baldy dove into the ditch beside the road as the final BANDALERO pulled his own pistol. Before he could fire it, Jason shot twice more, the rounds impacting less than an inch apart and both directly in the man's heart. The first BANDALERO was crawling toward his pistol in the road with blood pouring from his chest wound while he choked on even more pouring from his mouth and nose. With his last round, Jason fired into the man's head, ending the fight.

In an elapsed time of no more than ten seconds, four BANDALEROS lay dead on the gravel. Jason walked between two of the bodies, careful to avoid stepping in any blood and pulled the spark plug wires off one of the bikes. Tossing them to Baldy, he said, "Put these on and let's get the fuck outta here." He then picked all of his shell casings and hurried to his bike.

Baldy stood and looked at the spark plug wires in his hand. Then he looked at the carnage in the road. "Holy fucking shit!" he said in a voice that was barely above a whisper. "What the fuck just happened?" This last question was mostly to himself as he tried to get his drug and alcohol-clouded mind around the scene before him in the road.

"Baldy!" Jason yelled as he straddled his Road Glide. "Put the fucking wires on and let's get the fuck outta here! We can't afford to be fucking around, we gotta get, man!"

Baldy looked at Jason with a mixture of fear and uncertainty.

"Hey man, we should take their fucking wallets and guns."

"Fuck no! The longer we're here, the more likely we are to get busted. These broke-ass motherfuckers ain't got nothing anyway. That's why they were trying to rob us. Now let's get the fuck outta here. NOW damn it!"

Relenting, Baldy walked to his bike and put on the spark plug wires. In less than a minute, they were again running at nearly 100 miles per hour, heading to Sturgis.

Chapter 26

The next afternoon in Sturgis, the club officers all met in secret while the rest of the club stayed outside. After nearly an hour, Bull came out of the door and motioned for Jason to come into the room. As he entered, he saw everyone sitting or standing in semicircle in front of him. Lex was standing near the open door and said, "Baldy, wait outside while we talk to Jason."

"Why? As Road Captain, I'm an officer and I have a right to be here!" Baldy protested.

"I said get the fuck out! I'm not gonna tell you again. You're the worst fucking Road Captain in the history of the club, and it would be a pleasure to boot your sorry ass to the curb. Nobody likes getting lost every time we're more than twenty miles from home. Now get outside before I beat your ass and throw you out!"

"Fuck this shit," he said as he stood and walked toward the door. "This is some fucked up shit."

"Shut your fucking mouth asshole," Bull said as he grabbed Baldy by the back of his neck and shoved him down face first outside the room. Then he turned and closed the door.

Looking around the room, Lex's eyes settled on Jason. "We've got Baldy's version of what happened yesterday. We want you to tell us, so we can sort fact from fiction. Now starting with when you left Hulett, we need to know everything."

Jason was unsure what to say. He was still a Prospect, and the IRON KINGZ owed him nothing. Not loyalty. Not courtesy. Not friendship. And certainly not a cover-up for murder, even if it was just self-defense. He just stared at Lex and said nothing.

"Are you deaf? You need to tell us what happened. This is all private, and only the officers are here. Our "No Snitches" policy applies whenever we're doing club business, and this is definitely club business. I don't want to see my son go down as accessory to murder, and the club has to protect its own. Nobody else is going to help us, so we need to help ourselves. There's a news story out today that says four BANDALEROS were shot to death on a gravel road in Wyoming. Baldy says you two were there and it was self-defense. Is that the truth?"

"Pretty much."

Lex continued, prodding. "Baldy said it happened really fast. You stopped to work on his bike, these guys surrounded you, threatened you, pulled weapons, and got killed in the fight."

"That sounds about right."

"Baldy wasn't carrying a gun yesterday."

Jason said nothing. He just stared at Lex. The other officers were silent, listening to every word.

"Where was Baldy during the fight?"

"In the ditch beside the road."

"I gotta tell you Jason, I wouldn't normally believe one man could face four armed BANDALEROS and walk away without a scratch, but in this case, I don't doubt it. Now I'm gonna need you to step outside with the others, but before you go, I want to say thanks for what you did. Even if you had given those guys the money, they would have killed you anyway. You saved your own life and the life of a brother. Not just any brother, my son."

Jason did not respond but walked out the door. The rest of the club was milling around, some were working on bikes, some were smoking, others drinking. A couple were sleeping on their motorcycles with their heads on their luggage, and their feet over the handlebars. Baldy was off to one side, sitting on a curb alone. Jason turned and walked in the opposite direction of him. He found a Prospect working on his bike and stood next to him.

"What's going on in there?" the Prospect asked.

"You don't want to know, man."

Only a few minutes passed before Bull opened the door again and called all the Patches into the room except for Baldy. There was no protest this time. He just stayed where he was and hung his head low, embarrassed.

Nearly another hour passed while the entire club held their impromptu church. Jason eventually laid across his own bike and relaxed. It was getting hot, and he was tired of being out in the sun, uncertain what was going on behind closed doors.

Bull opened the door again and yelled, "Jason! Come back in here." He did not wait but left the door open and walked back into the crowded room. Jason entered and shut the door behind him. Every single person in the room had a deadly serious look on his face.

Lex spoke again. "Jason, I'm not going to fuck around with this anymore. What happened out there was serious business. Life and death business that affects the entire club. Since you've been Prospecting, you've done things that helped the club several times. Weapons, calling off the cops after Laconia, and now this. We met, we voted, and you're in!" With that he tossed Jason an IRON KINGZ rocker and full back patch, and everyone in the room cheered, clapped, shook his hand, hugged him, and welcomed him into the brotherhood.

Lex stepped forward with two smaller patches. The brothers got quiet as he handed them to Jason. The first was a Road Name patch. This would be what Jason would be called by the club members from now on. It was embroidered with the words FORTY-FIVE. "We had that one picked out a while back. Looks like we chose well," Lex said. Reaching out with the other patch, Jason saw that it was two crossed pistols. "Not too many guys get to wear this one. It's only given to guys who have killed for the club. Thanks again for saving Baldy. It looks like he didn't deserve to be saved, but I'm still glad you did."

Another round of handshakes, backslapping, and hugs broke out. Another round of beers was opened. Jason felt a kinship he had longed for, but had struggled to maintain his entire life. The football teams, the Marine Corps, the Highway Patrol; they were all in his past. Now he was an IRON KING, and he felt whole again.

"Get those fucking things sewn on tonight. We're leaving here tomorrow."

"You got it, Lex!"

When things quieted down a bit, Lex said, "We have one more bit of business to attend to. Your vote for membership wasn't the only vote we took." He motioned to Bull, who opened the door again and called Baldy into the room.

As Baldy entered, he looked angry, but Jason was certain he saw fear behind the anger. Everybody was quiet as church mice as Lex spoke. "Baldy, you have done nothing but fuck up on this trip. You've gotten the entire club lost every time we got on our bikes. You nearly got arrested in Hulett yesterday when you pulled that stupid shit. Then you nearly got killed. And honestly, if you hadn't had Jason with you, you would have gotten killed. We can overlook a lot of stupid shit, but when you hide in a fucking ditch while a Prospect fights for your life, you forfeit the right to wear the patch. Take it off. You're out."

Baldy turned as red as a beet, and the anger in his eyes turned to pure hatred. He looked around the room, but found no friends.

"Take off the cut," Lex repeated. "We're leaving tomorrow, but you won't be riding with us."

Baldy handed over his vest. He looked as lost and sad as any man Jason had ever seen.

Lex continued, "And if you utter so much as a peep to anybody, and I mean anybody on this planet about what happened out there yesterday, I will kill you myself."

With one last look over his shoulder, Baldy walked out the door and flipped the entire club the bird as he headed toward his old bike with the new spark plug wires.

Chapter 27

The next morning, Ratchet was involuntarily elected to the position of Road Captain. Lex's only words were, "Don't fuck this up and get us lost." Everybody laughed, and with that, the IRON KINGZ were on the road back to Tennessee. Jason rode with the main pack, glad to no longer have to bring up the rear with the other Prospects. His Road Glide was not yet one year old, but he already had nearly 30,000 miles on it. It was running better than ever, and Jason enjoyed the power he felt from it rolling along the highways. Riding amongst the club was loud - nobody had baffles in their exhaust pipes - but to Jason and the rest of the IRON KINGZ it was beautiful music.

Other traffic generally got out of the way of any large group of motorcycles, and when a band of 1%ers rolled through town, they were unmistakable. Their bikes were louder, much louder than a collection of citizen motorcycle enthusiasts. All the bikes had after-market handlebars. Most were ape hangers, but a few were very short, very narrow, or set very low on the bike. The bikers themselves took great pains to look different from the public. Long hair, long beards, tattoos and piercings were common. The public just wanted these guys out of their town, so they moved aside, and let them through. Jason liked that.

The ride home took a few days, and when they arrived, Jason attended his first official church. As the members sat at a large table in a room behind the bar at Ape-Hangers, the Prospects stood guard and tended the bar out front. Lex opened the meeting. "The only real business we need to settle tonight is what to do about re-establishing the IRON KINGZ in Delaware. Word has come down from National that our chapter will take the lead on dealing with the competition. We can use any members from other chapters that we need, and we have some great intel thanks to a couple of the Ol' Ladies who stayed behind. We know the two primary groups that pressured us out. One is a black gang called the Hood Rats, and the other is a chapter of another MC, the Low Lifes. We know where their clubhouses are, and we know when they meet. Any ideas?"

Bull was the first to speak. "Let's go in there and cut off their president's head. Those motherfuckers will back down after that."

"Let's burn their fucking clubhouses to the ground," offered Lefty.

Several patches spoke up in agreement with both suggestions, but Lex quieted the crowd. "We have twenty AKs. I am positive we have them outgunned. Does that change any minds?"

Jason spoke. "Lex, there's a smart way to do this. Here's my suggestion. We have twenty AKs. Let's put together a team of twenty guys. We can get some of the enforcers from our sister chapters. We can rent a couple of vans and go up there, not wearing our cuts, and not drawing any undue attention to the club. We can hit them at their meeting place while they're all there. I don't believe they will put up much of a fight against all our firepower. I believe we can make them surrender without firing a shot."

"Let's say that plan works. What do we do with them then?"

"We boot their asses outta town, and we're back in business. If we go in there and start shooting, or if we torch them, then there will be a lot more pressure for the cops to come after us. If we just quietly kick them out, then nobody really cares."

There was a long silence in the room. Everybody looked at Jason and Lex in an effort to see what they were thinking. Finally, Lex spoke. "If we go with your plan Forty-Five, I want you to lead it. I can sell this to National. Who do you want to go along?"

"I'll have a list to you by tomorrow. There are several guys from different chapters that have the skills I need. Young, strong, prior combat experience. I'll need a couple of weeks to organize all of it, but I think by mid-September we'll be back in business in Delaware with no competition."

Lex rapped the gavel on the table and smiled. "Done! Now let's get drunk."

Chapter 28

The next two weeks were busy for Jason. All the men he requested from the other chapters came to Paris, and they began to work in earnest. The Ol' Ladies in Delaware sent photos of the buildings where the rival clubs were headquartered. One even got pictures from the inside when she was invited to a party by a Prospect from the Low Lifes. The entire team studied these pictures and continued planning for the mission. It reminded Jason of the many times in Iraq that he was involved in setting up a combat operation. He treated it just like that, because in its essence, there was no difference.

The team went through several drills of entering rooms and clearing buildings. They all had military experience, and twelve of the twenty had been in actual combat. They understood the seriousness of what they were about to do, and they knew they only had one chance to get it right. The IRON KINGZ rented two cargo vans, and they practiced exiting the vans with the AKs and getting into a building quickly.

News came from an Ol' Lady in Delaware that one of the Hood Rats died in a car wreck. The funeral was in two days, and the Hood Rats planned to hold a party in his memory that night in their clubhouse. The Low Lifes were holding church the same night. Jason met with the team to discuss this development.

"Ok guys, the less time we're in town, the less likely we are to draw attention. Just like we have planned and rehearsed. We split into two groups of ten. One van goes to the Low Lifes' clubhouse and catches them during church. The other van goes to the Hood Rats clubhouse at the same time and catches them during their party. Remember, we don't want to pull the trigger unless we absolutely have to. We're not trying to kill them. We're trying to put the fear of God in them, and let them know that we mean business."

Bull spoke up. "I assume you'll lead one of the teams. Who's going to lead the other?"

Jason looked around at the group. They were all hard men. Good fighters. Good with weapons. One stood out, a big man and former Army Ranger from the Orlando Chapter. His name was Scarface, not just because of the long scar running from his ear to his mouth, the result of a knife fight in 1991 during the first Gulf War, but because he was Cuban as well. His vest included the crossed pistol patch. Looking closely in his eyes, Jason said, "Scarface, you up to it?"

"You bet Forty-Five. I can do it. Which club am I taking down?"

"I think I'll send you after the Low Lifes. Let's talk later and divide up the men."

"Good enough."

"All right then" Jason said. "All of you make your last minute preparations, and we will leave here at 7 a.m. tomorrow. My plan is to get there, do our business, and get out all in one day. National has the new chapter members lined up to come in and take over as soon as we disappear."

As the others filed away to take care of their personal business, Scarface stayed behind and worked out the final preparations with Jason. Team assignments were made and all the smallest details were double and triple-checked before they went home to rest before the long day ahead.

The next morning dawned bright and clear. All the men showed up ready for the ride to Delaware. As they traveled, each leader discussed the plan with his team. Mentally rehearsing the attack and discussing how to handle countless different scenarios that might arise during its execution. It was well after dark when the vans pulled into Dover and refueled for the getaway. Jason and Scarface each addressed the teams one final time before heading to their separate locations.

The two clubhouses were only a few blocks apart, but were located in the slummiest neighborhood in Dover. The IRON KINGZ' abandoned clubhouse was about halfway between them. Jason still felt responsible for Scarface and his team, but he needed to focus all his attention on the task in front of him. The Hood Rats were known to be a violent and dangerous gang, but he hoped that catching them drunk, high, and mourning the loss of one of their own would give him all the advantage he needed. As the van approached the address, all the men double-checked their rifles and readied themselves for a fight.

There were two black teenagers standing in front of the clubhouse as the van screeched to a halt on the sidewalk in front of them and the doors opened revealing the heavily-armed bikers. Neither had a chance to react before they felt rifle butts pounding them over and over. The street was otherwise deserted as the bikers entered the building, leaving the two incapacitated guards lying on the sidewalk. One man stood in the open door to cover the backs of his brothers while they were inside.

Inside, rap music blared from a nightclub-quality sound system. The bikers spread out around the perimeter of the room yelling for everyone to get on the ground and beating anyone who was slow to obey. Within moments, several members of the Hood Rats were bleeding and unconscious on the floor. The lights came on as the music shut off. About forty men and women, all black, and all under thirty years old, were lying down as Jason took charge. "Who's the fucking president here? I want an answer now, or we're gonna start shooting you one at a time until I get a name!"

There was only a momentary silence before a well-built man in his mid-twenties rose to his feet and said defiantly, "That's me. What you motha fuckers want?"

Jason walked over to him and snatched him forward by his collar. Once he was off-balance, Jason shoved the muzzle of the AK into his throat. "Listen to me motherfucker. The Hood Rats are done here. Do you fucking understand me? You fucked with the IRON KINGZ and that was a big fucking mistake. You have two choices. You can end this shit right here and now and walk away, or we can kill everybody in this room and then kill anybody else who ain't here as soon as we see them on the street. Either way, you're fucking done. It's your choice, MAKE IT NOW!"

"Fuck you bitch!" was the only reply. The words barely escaped his lips however, before Rat broke three of the man's ribs with one stroke from his rifle butt. He sank to his knees, coughing up blood, but Jason never let go of his collar and jerked him back to his feet. The pain was evident on his face as Jason jammed the muzzle back under his chin.

"Motherfucker, I'm gonna give you one chance to reconsider and save the lives of everybody else here." As he spoke these words, a loud thud resounded from across the room, followed by a groan. Another gang member had tried to pull a pistol, but a biker saw it and landed a hard stomp to the man's head, smashing his face into the floor. "Tell these stupid motherfuckers not to try that shit again. We're in charge here. Do you understand me bitch?"

The president nodded his head. A small trickle of blood oozed from the corner of his mouth. His eyes were wide with pain and fear.

"Now what's it gonna be?" Jason asked one final time as he pressed the muzzle more tightly into the man's throat.

"We quit," was the hoarsely whispered reply.

Jason spun him around and held the muzzle to the back of his head. "Everybody look at me!" he yelled. Heads and eyes all over the room turned to see him. Some were terrified, others were enraged, but everybody stayed on the ground. "Say it again! Tell everybody what you just told me. I want them to hear it from you."

In a voiced tinged with pain but loud enough for everybody, the president said, "We quit."

Jason slammed him face first into the floor and looked around the room. "You heard him!" he yelled. "The Hood Rats are out of business. If you fuck with another IRON KING, I promise you we will hunt your ass down and kill you as dead as a motherfucker. Do not fucking test us. We own this fucking town now, and you motherfuckers better make yourselves scarce after we leave."

With that, the bikers hurried out the door and sped away. At a gas station outside of town on a small highway, they met with Scarface and his team. They had successfully disbanded the Low Lifes and had not had to fire a shot either. Jason made a phone call to National to let them know that the situation was handled and that it was safe for the new Delaware club chapter to roll into town to reoccupy the old clubhouse. Jason and company headed back to Tennessee, but not before stocking up on beer for the trip. The road party was a good one and lasted until they pulled into Paris around noon the following day.

Chapter 29

Rat moved back to Delaware, and for the next two years, things were quiet for the IRON KINGZ. Jason continued his import business, and relaxed in a comfortable life. There had been enough drama for a while, and the entire club was taking a much-needed breather. By the summer of 2008, the outlook for the IRON KINGZ was very promising.

When the Delaware Chapter took over the operations of the Hood Rats and the Low Lifes, it came with a significant drug trade in Dover. Rat had advanced this business with a method that was similar to Jason's. He had contacted a Pakistani national whom he had met near the border with Afghanistan and was importing pure heroin. The profits from this were astounding and it was not long before the money became almost impossible to launder. They had to funnel it out of Delaware, and spread it among the other club chapters. Using the legitimate businesses owned by other club members to cover the money trail, new clubhouses were built with cash and new motorcycles purchased.

Jason turned down all money the club offered. As he watched the opulence the bikers were suddenly enjoying, he knew it would not be long before it caught the attention of the cops. He needed to distance himself from the bust he knew must be coming. Pleading with Lex and the other members of his own chapter, he told them repeatedly that they were in serious trouble if they kept it up. Flush with cash they never experienced before in their lives, the bikers ignored him and continued their lavish spending. Lex rebuilt his bar and even put up a new house for himself on the property.

Parties at sister chapters had become commonplace as most members did not really have to work for a living anymore, but preferred to ride, and where better to ride than to see their brothers in another state? Whenever the Delaware and Tennessee chapters got together, Jason got more and more concerned about Rat. Every time they met, Rat was a little more strung out on the dope that was making him rich. As the addiction increased, his judgment decreased. Still, a club member's business was his business, so Jason never spoke up.

That changed one night in early October when the Delaware chapter visited Paris.

As the party raged, Jason and Julie came into Ape-Hangers and got a beer from the bar. Club members never paid. That was just for other customers in Lex's legitimate business. They took seats at a table with a couple of the brothers from Delaware and their Ol' Ladies. Within a few minutes Rat came over and said "Hey Forty-Five, I want to introduce you to our new Prospect. Prospect Eddie, meet Forty-Five."

Jason's heart stopped for a brief second. Prospect Eddie was a familiar face. The long, stringy blonde hair was unmistakable, and the tired look in the eyes was the same as the last time Jason had seen him.

Prospect Eddie was Special Agent Tyler from the DEA.

He had run the undercover drug operation Jason supported when he was still with the Highway Patrol nearly three years before. Now he was back on a new assignment, and although Jason knew that Prospect Eddie would never recognize him with his shaved head and twelve-inch braided goatee, he also knew that Prospect Eddie's presence could only mean one thing: the IRON KINGZ were being targeted by the DEA.

Jason nodded at the new Prospect, but did not shake his hand. This was a common move between a Patch and a Prospect, and allowed Jason to keep some distance. "Nice to meet you, Forty-Five".

"Yeah." Jason returned to his conversation at the table, and Rat moved on to another area to continue the introductions. Jason's mind was racing. He could not allow his brothers to be busted by the DEA, but if he announced who Prospect Eddie really was, the IRON KINGZ would kill the agent right then. There seemed to be no way out. He excused himself, told Julie to go hang out with the other Ol' Ladies, and walked out on the large front porch to think while he sipped his Budweiser and looked at the bikes.

Were there other undercover agents? How deep did this go? What did Prospect Eddie know? How long had he been hanging around the Delaware Chapter? Had he found the evidence to tie the drug money to the whole club?

Probably so. That would be easy. There was just too much of it to hide, and the club had not been smart about trying to hide it. They spent money like lottery winners with no regard for who might notice. That was how the DEA noticed them in the first place. An undercover investigation with an agent actually Prospecting in a 1%er club was long and expensive. It had likely been going on for more than a year. Perhaps even as far back as the night of the Delaware raids. If word had gotten out about twenty IRON KINGZ armed with AKs shutting down two rival clubs in one night that would certainly get some attention in law enforcement circles.

As Jason was mulling this over, the front door opened and Prospect Eddie came outside. He and Jason were alone on the front porch, and Jason motioned for him to come over. He knew the operation had likely already netted enough information to get some indictments, but the longer it went on, the more serious the charges would get. As Prospect Eddie approached, Jason leaned forward, looked him in the eye from less than three inches away, and whispered in a strong voice, "I know who you are. I know what you're doing. If I tell those guys inside, you'll be dead before you can get to your bike or your backup can get here. Here's your one chance at life: get on your bike, leave, and don't ever come around one of my brothers again. This investigation is over, and if you ever come back, I'll kill you myself. Got it?"

Fear flashed across Prospect Eddie's face. It quickly melted to some relief when Jason gave him the option to leave. Now that he was outed, the investigation was over anyway, but he would at least get away with his life. That was rare for an exposed undercover agent, and he knew it. Within seconds, his Softail Springer came alive and he was rolling down the highway. Jason went back inside, stayed just long enough for some key people to see he was still there, told Lex he had to get to Atlanta on business, grabbed Julie, and they mounted his bike and left.

Jason returned to Paris a few days later, and overheard some of the guys still wondering what had happened to the Prospect from Delaware. He disappeared during the party, and had not been heard from since. His apartment in Dover was empty, and nobody could explain his absence. Apparently, he had been a good Prospect who helped move a lot of heroin, and was likely on the fast track to getting patched in. But now he was gone. Jason knew if they ever saw Prospect Eddie again, he would not be on a motorcycle and the vest he wore would be bulletproof.

Chapter 30

As winter came and the temperatures dropped in Tennessee, Jason made an announcement during church that he was going to visit the Alabama Chapter in Mobile for a few months. It was much warmer down there, and he could still run his Atlanta business with ease. Lex and the rest of the members gave their blessing and the following week Jason said goodbye to Julie and was southbound on Alabama backroads. His Road Glide was laden with everything he needed to enjoy a few months in the Deep South. The Colt .45 tucked into his back was purchased new after the shooting in Sturgis two years earlier. He melted the murder weapon from that trip with a blowtorch as soon as he got back to town.

Approaching Mobile on Highway 13 South, he was passing through Wagarville when he saw the blue lights of a local police car approaching fast behind him. His IRON KINGZ vest was on full display, and he was close enough to Mobile that the local Wagarville Police were probably aware of the club and its nature.

He pulled over near a driveway, shut the bike off, and lowered his kickstand. The officer who emerged from the car could not have been more than 22 years old. "This young punk probably doesn't even shave yet," he thought to himself as he fingered his own beard.

"Do you know what the speed limit is through here?" asked the rookie from a few feet behind Jason.

"No, but I'm sure you'll tell me" came the reply with only a hint of sarcasm.

"It's 35. Do you know how fast you were going?"

"Well, if the speed limit is 35, then I must have been going 35."

"I clocked you at 42 passing that intersection back there. Can I see your license and registration?"

"It's in my hip pocket. Can I reach in there to get it?" the question was rhetorical, but Jason knew this rookie probably thought he had a major felon on his hands, so he was unpredictable, and Jason was in no mood to go to jail on some trumped up charge. The fact of the matter was, ironically, that this rookie actually had an international arms trafficker stopped on the roadside in this sleepy Alabama town, but he had no clue about that, and he would not be learning any more about it today. Jason handed over the documents from his wallet, and watched as the officer walked backwards to his patrol car's door and climbed inside.

Forty-two in a thirty-five would not normally warrant a second look, but when the officer is a rookie who wants to make a name for himself, and the speeder is a patched member of a outlaw motorcycle club, it's a recipe for a stop anytime. Jason had been through this a dozen times over the last couple of years. He no longer had any patience with cops that only wanted to send the message, "Stay out of my town." The officer got out of his car and walked back up to Jason. He was not carrying any of the paperwork. "Mr. Broaduc, can you step away from your motorcycle please?"

"Sure," Jason spat the reply while glaring at the officer with utter disdain.

"I would like for you to take a seat over here on the curb. Are you carrying anything illegal today? Drugs? Missile launchers? Anything at all?"

Jason had a permit to carry his .45 that was valid in several states, including Alabama, so he was not even lying when he answered, "No," and sat down on the curb.

"Then you won't mind if I have a look?"

"Actually, I mind very much. I'm not going to consent to any searches," he answered without taking his eyes from the rookie.

"But if you don't have..."

Jason cut him off and said, "I told you I'm not consenting to any searches. Now that ends that. Go write your ticket if you want to, but don't ask me about searching anything again!"

Anger flashed in the rookie's eyes. Still, his voice remained relatively calm, even condescending. "All I need is probable cause, and I can search anything I want, asshole. If you have anything illegal, you need to tell me now."

Jason chuckled out loud. "I already told you I don't have anything illegal. I also told you I'm not consenting to any searches. There is no point in arguing. You don't have probable cause to search, and I'm not consenting."

The rookie's face turned red as he stared hard and cold at Jason.

"Don't move" he said as walked backward toward his car once again. Jason watched the passing traffic as he sat and waited for the officer to emerge from his vehicle again. Nearly thirty minutes expired before that happened. Apparently the wheels of justice turn a little slower in Wagarville. "Mr. Broaduc, I need you to sign here" he said before letting Jason go with the speeding ticket. "Try to keep it a little slower next time."

Jason did not utter a word. He got on his bike, and pulled back out onto the highway with dreams of cold beer and brotherhood burning in his mind.

⟺•⟺

The IRON KINGZ were all drinking at the Mobile clubhouse when Jason pulled up and parked amid the row of Harleys. Hugs and backslaps were exchanged all around as he settled into the bar. Two girlfriends of members, wearing only their panties, were grinding against each other on the elevated dance floor, complete with a pole. "So how's everything in Tennessee?" asked Gator, the Mobile chapter President.

"Same as always. Lex and the other brothers send their regards. Cold as fuck up there. I think I'm gonna get an apartment here for the winter."

"Sounds good to me," replied Gator as a Prospect came up with two more cold beers. After handing them to the bikers, he melted away into the crowd. "I got a friend; he owns an extended-stay place. Kinda like a small apartment, but with maid service. I can get him to hook you up if you want."

"Hell yeah. That'll work just fine!" Jason took a long pull from the Budweiser bottle. He looked at the two women on the dance floor, and it reminded him of something else he would need during the chilly nights on the Gulf Coast while Julie was still in Tennessee. "Are the maids there good-looking?" he asked, smiling.

"Fuck no! They're all old, fat, and black! If you need a woman though, just say the word, we can hook you up with that too."

"No thanks. I believe I can find plenty of that on my own. Old skanks ain't really my thing."

"I hear that," said Gator, raising his bottle to toast Jason. "Seems like I remember you having a pretty young thing in Paris. I guess she didn't make the trip?"

Jason completed the toast and said, "Julie? Nah. She does her thing, I do mine. We hook up pretty often, ride with the club, whatever. But there's nothing serious about it."

"Good man," said Gator. "Come to church tomorrow night. If you're gonna be here for a while, you might as well be in touch with what's going on."

"Wouldn't miss it for the world."

Chapter 31

Jason drank beer with the Mobile brothers until the wee hours of the morning. He slept in one of the bedrooms at the clubhouse. The next morning he was pouring coffee in the kitchen area while a Prospect was cleaning up from the night before. It was raining outside, and with his hangover, Jason was not feeling very cheerful. The prospect turned on a vacuum cleaner and Jason yelled, "Hey Prospect! Turn that fucking thing off! For God's sake, at least let me get some coffee and some Motrin before you start making all that racket."

"No problem, Forty Five," came the humble reply as the Prospect went away to clean something a little quieter. Jason sat on a couch and thumbed through the television channels. A local morning news broadcast was airing a story about a motorcycle rally scheduled in Mobile that weekend. They interviewed a couple of the early arrivals. Stunned, Jason stared at the screen and watched the man being interviewed. It was none other than Captain Stan Tucker, his nemesis from the highway patrol days, in town on his shiny new Honda Goldwing and ready to enjoy the weekend.

Jason's anger rose as he watched the Captain smugly recount for the reporter that this weekend's focus would be on motorcycle safety and family fun. "This is not a bike rally with a bunch of hoodlums on Harleys. This is a bunch of family-friendly, good American citizens who enjoy riding our motorcycles, but not with exhaust pipes loud enough to annoy people. We invite anyone to come down to the park and enjoy the weekend with us, whether you ride a motorcycle or not."

Jason nearly choked on his coffee as he thought back to the arrogance and outright abuse he had suffered through while working for this man. "'Hoodlums on Harleys' my ass," he thought. "I got something for you."

Before church let out, Jason took the floor. "What do y'all know about this rice-burner rally in the park this weekend?" he asked the group.

When the IRON KINGZ gathered for church that night, Gator reintroduced Jason to the chapter. They again welcomed him like the brother he was. Jason had taken a room in the extended stay motel on the outskirts of town earlier in the day. Gator's friend was not a brother, but was a friend to the club. When he had some tenants who were not paying a few years before, the club took care of the problem. As repayment, he let IRON KINGZ stay at his motel free of charge whenever they needed some time away from their Ol' Ladies, or wanted to be with another woman their Ol' Ladies did not know about. He refused Jason's offer of cash for the room, insisting that no IRON KING would ever pay to stay there. Reluctantly, Jason agreed.

Before church let out, Jason took the floor. "What do y'all know about this rice-burner rally in the park this weekend?" he asked the group.

"Not much. I think it moves locations every year. This year just happens to be in Mobile. Why?"

"Well, I saw a story about it on the news this morning. They interviewed a guy, and this motherfucker was my old boss. He tried to ruin my life, and I'm lucky I didn't do any time when he was done fucking me. I haven't seen him since, but I think this might be a good opportunity for me to get a little payback. He was talking about the family-friendly bullshit all those Jap-bikers do, but it's a public event in a public park. We could ruin his whole weekend just by showing up."

Gator looked around the room. "Anybody got any plans for the weekend better than fucking over this asshole?" Heads shook all around, and evil smiles abounded among the eight bikers. "Well then, I guess we got ourselves a party!"

⟫⟪◍⟫⟪

The next morning dawned a bright, crisp, and comfortable 70 degrees. Not a cloud hung in the sky. The Gulf of Mexico beckoned with gentle waves as the IRON KINGZ rolled into Hughes Park, opposite the beach on Highway 90. The outlaws gunned the engines on their Harley Davidsons in the park that was otherwise filled with quiet-running Hondas and Kawasakis. Finding a spot in a large parking lot near a makeshift stage that served as the hub of the weekend's activity, the 1%ers parked and dismounted, their leather cuts with the three-piece patches causing a stir among the locals and "civilized" motorcycle enthusiasts. One young mother pushing a stroller quickly turned and hurried in the opposite direction as they climbed from their bikes.

Gator spoke loudly. "Okay boys! Let's see what's going on at this MO-TOR-SICK-EL event!" He stressed every syllable of the word as if the only real motorcycles in the park belonged to the club.

A couple of men from a nearby group left their wives and children and approached the IRON KINGZ. Jason gave his brothers a look that said, "Neither of these two is our guy, so let's play it cool for now." They returned his glance in acknowledgement.

"Hey guys," one of the men said as they neared the bikers, "I'm Tommy Wendt. This is my riding partner James Curtis." Both men smiled and extended their hands to shake with the group. None of the bikers moved or spoke. None accepted the outstretched hands. They looked hard at the two men, and after a brief moment, the hands were lowered.

"Is there something we can help you with?" asked Gator, the sarcasm in his voice obvious.

"Look guys," Tommy spoke as he nervously glanced back over his shoulder, "we don't want any trouble. This is a friendly event." James had already taken a step back from Tommy and was looking around uncomfortably for support from anywhere. There was none to be had.

"Yeah, we know it's a friendly event. What makes you think we ain't friendly?" Gator laughed as he looked at his brothers. A couple smiled, the rest never took their hard eyes off the duo in front of them. "We're just here to have a good time. Same as you. Now you go on about your business, and we'll go on about ours."

Tommy and James wasted no time in beating a hasty retreat once the door was opened. The IRON KINGZ laughed amongst themselves and, staying in a group, began walking among the many vendors in the park. It was not yet 11:00 but a couple of the outlaws stopped by a concession selling beer along with its other fare, mostly hamburgers, giant pretzels, and funnel cakes. "Give us a twelve pack of Budweiser!" one yelled through the sliding window at the young clerk, a teen-aged girl who looked like she had seen a monster.

Her voice cracked, "Sir, we can't serve beer until noon. I'm sorry."

Hothead, the large, bearded, unbathed biker turned back towards his brothers and screamed loud enough for half the park to hear. "Do you believe this shit? These motherfuckers don't sell beer until noon. Gator, I didn't know you were bringing us to the Land of Pussies!"

All the IRON KINGZ laughed loudly and continued on through the park. Hothead turned back to the girl and threw a five dollar bill through the open window. "Keep that, you pretty thing. I'll be back at noon for my beer." He smiled and walked off to join his posse while retrieving a flask from his pocket and taking a long pull of straight bourbon. The young girl picked up the money between her thumb and forefinger like it was contaminated and dropped it into the tip jar. Her lip curled in disgust at having touched it, and fear was still in her eyes.

And so it continued throughout the remainder of the morning, the IRON KINGZ intimidating virtually anyone who crossed their path, while Jason constantly scanned the crowd for any sign of his quarry. In the back of his mind, he knew that as long as the IRON KINGZ continued to make their presence known, Tucker would eventually turn up, and he hoped the man would be looking for a fight. He was likely to find one either way.

Hughes Park was not that large, and within two hours, the IRON

KINGZ had perused all the wares from the vendors and made their way back toward the stage where a three-piece band was setting up. The parking lot in front of their bikes was a hub of activity, with volunteers setting out small cones, outlining the obstacles for the bike games scheduled for later in the day. The Prospects watching over the IRON KINGZ' bikes saw the group approaching and one walked up to Gator. "Hey Prez," he began, "some guy came up and said when the bike games start, we were going to have to move. I told him I would discuss it with you when you got back. He flashed a badge and said it was either move or be towed. I said 'Fuck you' and he walked off. Just thought you should know."

Jason was standing next to Gator as the Prospect relayed this news. "Where's the dumbass who said that?" he asked.

"The guy wearing the reflective yellow jacket standing next to the maroon Goldwing." The Prospect pointed to the far end of the lot.

Jason recognized Tucker immediately, even from across the large parking lot. "Good. That's the son-of-a-bitch I wanted to see. Get back to the bikes, Prospect. I want to talk to Gator." The Prospect turned on his heels and hustled back down to the group of Harley Davidson motorcycles.

"Hey Gator," Jason said, "I say we go down to the bikes and just hang out. Have the Prospects go buy some beer and bring it to us. That arrogant motherfucker will come back over to start his shit and start flashing his badge. Let me handle him."

"Works for me, Forty-Five. It's your beef, but we got your back. This has been pretty fun anyway." Gator smiled, and Jason knew he was enjoying himself. Intimidation was an IRON KINGZ trademark. Turning back to the group, Gator spoke loudly enough for others nearby to hear. "Hey guys, we're going back down to the bikes, maybe listen to this pussy band for a while. Hothead, send the Prospects back to your girlfriend to get us some beer. Don't go yourself. Send the Prospects. If you go, God knows you'll probably be in jail for rape before the beer has a chance to get warm."

All the IRON KINGZ laughed, including Hothead. "No problem Boss," he said as his face turned bright red beneath his unkempt beard.

As the 1%ers walked toward their motorcycles, Jason saw Tucker look up and notice them. "It won't be long now, jackass," he thought. "You're gonna get yours today."

As the preparations in the parking lot continued and the band started into their first set, a bluesy folk rock tune, the Prospects returned with a full case of beer. "Some old fucker was at the stand. The girl was gone. He said he wasn't supposed to 'sell beer in bulk'. I laughed in his face, and told him he could either sell it in bulk, or we'll take it in bulk, but either way we were leaving there with a case of beer. He saw it our way." Everyone laughed a little louder than necessary at the story.

Jason looked up to see Captain Tucker and three other men he did not recognize approaching the bikes. "Hey!" Tucker yelled at the assembled IRON KINGZ as the first tops were cracked on the Budweisers. "Who's in charge here?" His voice was authoritative; an effort to let the bikers know that whoever claimed to be in charge would soon be answering to him.

"That's me," Gator said before anyone else could speak. The entire group turned toward the approaching men. Silence hung in the air, even the band, between two songs, was quiet, listening.

Tucker spoke to Gator, but everyone was watching closely. "Well, you need to get your guys, and get your bikes, and move on. You can't be here when the games start, and frankly, I don't like the way you're acting anyway. This is a family event, and you're nothing but in our way." The men had stopped in the lot just short of the line of Harleys, while the bikers stood on grass beyond the pavement. The bikes stood like a barrier between the two groups and the tension in the air was electric.

"Is that a fact?" Gator asked, stepping forward slightly. "It looks like a public park, and a public parking lot to me. Maybe you need to move your stupid-ass games somewhere else."

Tucker produced his badge and repeated, "I'll have every one of these oil-leaking pieces of shit towed out of here. If you think I'm playing, just try me."

Jason stepped forward and spoke. "I didn't know the Tennessee Highway Patrol had the authority to do that in Alabama," he said. Tucker looked at him as if he were seeing someone he should know, but could not place. Jason looked quite different in his IRON KINGZ cut, with his long goatee, plus it had now been three years since the two had seen each other. He continued, "You got nothing, and you know it. You and your butt-buddies can just get the fuck away from us. We ain't moving."

"The hell you aren't!" Tucker yelled as he moved between two Harleys closing the gap with Jason. In the process, he stumbled over a kickstand and caught his balance by grabbing a set of ape hangers.

"What the fuck?" Jason screamed only inches from the Tucker's face. "You never touch another man's bike, you stupid fuck!" Jason towered over the man, but the bravado of having bullied the public and his fellow troopers for so long was not so quickly quelled in Tucker. He shoved Jason in the chest, but succeeded in moving him only a couple of inches. While Tucker's hands were still on his chest, Jason grabbed the smaller man by his throat with his left hand and lifted him onto his tiptoes. The grip was like iron, and Tucker flailed momentarily at Jason's wrist but soon saw the fruitlessness of his efforts. He reached toward his jacket pocket and Jason knew he was going for a gun. In a flash, Jason jerked him to the ground like a ragdoll and brought a crushing knee into his face. A sickening crunch rang out as Tucker's cheekbone failed and he lapsed into unconsciousness. Jason reached into Tucker's jacket pocket and pulled the .38 caliber snub-nosed Smith and Wesson revolver out. "Is this what you're looking for dumbass?" he asked. Standing over the downed man, Jason emptied the shells from the gun into his hand and dropped the revolver to the ground beside the humiliated Tennessee Highway Patrol Captain.

The other men with Tucker had backed away, and one of them was on his cell phone with 911. Looking at Gator, Jason said, "I think our business here is done."

Gator and the others were all smiles as they rode away from the park, kicking every biker-game cone away as they passed.

Jason realized that for the first time in a long time that he fought and his world had not gone red. He thought, "There's something to be said for the healing qualities of brotherhood."

Chapter 32

The rest of the winter passed quietly for the IRON KINGZ in Mobile. Jason made his Atlanta run every month, ever more careful each time that he was not being followed. He knew the DEA was onto the drug connections for the club, and it was just a matter of time before the bust came. The money was continuing to flow freely among all the chapters, and he tried to distance himself from it as much as possible. He repeatedly warned everyone in the club that there was no way to continue their lifestyles without catching the attention of the law. His pleas either fell on deaf ears or he was given only minor attention. With half the club using hard drugs and having more cash available than they ever dreamed possible, they were simply unprepared to listen, even to sage advice.

In February, Rat and the rest of the Delaware Chapter members came to Mobile to escape the cold of the north. As soon as Jason saw Rat, he knew the former Marine was in serious trouble. Rail-thin with bags under his cold and empty eyes and track marks from injections in every conceivable vein in his arms, Rat looked like the walking dead. Pulling him aside one morning while he was still semi-sober, Jason confronted him. "You look like shit, brother. What the fuck has happened to you? You gotta stop this shit and get off the hard stuff. It's killing you quick."

Rat's eyes were deep pockets of black, like a bottomless pit into a soul that no longer existed. "I don't know, man. I think I got this under control. I can stop whenever I want. There's just no reason to quit. Everybody likes it. It's making us a shitload of money."

Jason interrupted and grabbed Rat by the shoulders. "Listen motherfucker! You're out of your mind. I don't want to see anybody in this club go down. You're all my brothers, but you were a fucking Marine! You know better than this shit! Let me take you out of here for a while. We can go somewhere and let you dry out. It will probably do us both a lot of good. If you don't, you're not gonna last."

"Hey man, listen. There is absolutely no fucking way I'm going to leave here and go anywhere. I told you I got it under control. Now fuck off and mind your own business." Rat tried to pull away, but the much larger and stronger Jason held him fast.

"Dude, the Feds are coming and soon. It would be a lot better for you if you had a clear mind to deal with them. I don't know what's happened to this club. Everybody's got their heads so far up their asses; they haven't seen daylight in forever. Nobody wants to listen to the fact that there's no way they can keep this up without getting busted."

The two Marines stared intently into each other's faces for a long and uncomfortable moment. Rat said, "Listen, if the fucking Feds come after me, it's gonna look like the last scene in Scarface. Those fuckers better bring their A-game."

"Listen to yourself!" Jason pleaded. "There's no way you can win that. They will kill you and then go about their day like nothing happened!"

"If that happens, then fuck it. At least I had a good ride." His eyes softened slightly and a bit of life could be seen deep within. "Listen bro, I know you're right, but I don't see any way out of this. I know we fucked it up, but you're a smart motherfucker. You could have done it better, and the IRON KINGZ would be better off if we had listened to you. It's too late now. I hope you don't have to go down with us, and if you get away, then you can still ride for all of us. You'll be National President of the IRON KINGZ one day, I know it. You're too fucking smart not to. You can do it better than we did. At the farthest corner of the fence behind my place in Delaware, there's a box buried about two feet deep. It's got all the information you need to restart the trade, and do it right."

"Fuck that shit!" Jason yelled. "I don't want anything to do with that. You need to start thinking straight, motherfucker."

Rat pulled away and walked back toward the club. "Sorry man. That's all I got."

Jason watched him go. He felt nothing but pity and fear for the IRON KINGZ. He wanted to see these men succeed. They had been by his side through some tough times, and had never shown him anything but total loyalty. He knew most of them would take a bullet for him, and he feared that just might happen if they did not change their ways soon.

———◦《◉》◦———

As spring approached, Jason went back to Paris and resettled into his life. He was helping Lex and the rest of the club prepare for the annual run to Myrtle Beach Bike Week in May. At church, Stoner reported that the national officers had reserved an entire floor of the Hilton for the club. He had paid the Tennessee chapter's share out of the petty cash fund. Jason laughed to himself and thought, "Since when did $12,000 constitute petty cash? I guess it seems that way when you're high as a kite most of the time."

As church broke up, Lex said, "Hey Forty-Five. I need to talk to you for a minute."

"Sure Lex. What's up?"

Lex closed the door as the last member left the room, and he and Jason stood alone. "You've been pretty hard on the club for our spending habits. You've refused to take even a dime of the money for yourself, even though it's been offered many times. If I didn't know better, I would think you were working with the Feds. I just don't see a narc trying to get us out of the business though, so I know you're righteous."

He continued, "I'm old, and I've seen better days. I remember when this club consisted of five members nationally. Now we have several hundred. I remember when the whole club couldn't scrape together enough money to take a weekend ride. Now we're renting entire floors of five-star hotels. It doesn't make sense to me how we did it, but it's done. I know it's probably too late for most of us. The thing that bothers me the most is seeing so many brothers strung out on the very shit that made us all rich."

"I said all that to say this; nobody knows, but I have Stage Five lung cancer. The doc says I have less than six months to live. Now I don't want anybody to know about that." He stared with ice-cold eyes at Jason long enough to get an acknowledgment. "I believe you when you say we're all about to get busted. I should have done something about it a long time ago, but I was enjoying the money too much. Now that I know I'm dying, I have a different perspective. The IRON KINGZ have been good to me, and I don't want to see them die when I do. If anybody escapes when the Feds come, it will be you. Promise me that you won't let the IRON KINGZ die. Promise me you will take the club and bring it back."

Jason looked at Lex, but then dropped his gaze to the floor. Looking back up after a moment, he stared his club president, mentor, sponsor, and surrogate father in the eyes. "I'll do my best Lex. You know I love the IRON KINGZ, and it kills me that it's come to this, but I'll do everything I can to make it right."

Chapter 33

The bust finally came early on a Wednesday morning in late April. Agents from virtually every federal law enforcement agency, supported by state and local police swarmed over every clubhouse, personal residence, and other hangout for every member of the IRON KINGZ nationally. It was the largest coordinated federal sting ever executed. The Director of Homeland Security reported on the morning news that over 200 IRON KINGZ were taken into custody on charges ranging from simple possession to conspiracy to distribute narcotics, and even domestic terrorism. He went on to say the organization had been one of the largest suppliers of narcotics in the United States, and that this was the greatest victory to date in the War on Drugs. The Attorney General announced that he intended to prosecute the charges under the RICO statutes, which allowed everyone connected to the club to be charged with all the crimes as a group.

For Jason, it came at 4:02 a.m. when the battering ram hit the doorknob on his front door, smashing it in and waking him from an unfinished night's sleep. As he reached for his pistol on the nightstand, he heard the shouts of "Police! Search Warrant!" and put the weapon down. He sat up on the bed and put his hands behind his head only seconds before a half-dozen police dressed in full SWAT gear and carrying automatic rifles entered his room. Despite not resisting, the officers took him to the floor hard and even landed a few gratuitous punches and kicks before cuffing him and leading him outside into the cool morning air. As two men put him in the back of the squad car, at least a dozen more began ransacking his house, looking for evidence of his criminal connections. He knew they would find nothing they could use, and he was glad Julie was at her own house that day. She did not need to be caught up in this.

Jason, aka Forty-Five, was booked at the Henry County Jail on charges of conspiracy to distribute narcotics and held without bail. The other IRON KINGZ from the Tennessee Chapter were housed there as well, though they were all kept in individual cells and not allowed to communicate with anyone but guards.

Forty-eight hours later, a guard led Jason to a small room with only a table and two chairs. A two-way mirror adorned one wall, and two cameras with their red "Record" lights blinking preserved the sights and sounds. He sat alone, handcuffed to the chair for several minutes before the door opened and an all-too-familiar face entered. His hair was cut, and he looked much healthier than either other time Jason had seen him, but Special Agent Tyler was still very recognizable.

"Good morning Jason." The agent spoke in a friendly voice. "Or do you prefer to be called Forty-Five?"

Jason sat silently. He had not spoken to anyone since his arrest, and he did not intend to start now. The right to remain silent was his primary defense.

"Well," Tyler continued as he took a seat across the table, "I was warned that you were not talking, and that's fine with me. I just have some things to say to you, and then I'll be on my way. Capiche?"

Silence.

Turning to the cameras, Agent Tyler stood and walked first to one and then to the other and unplugged them both. The flashing red lights went dark. "Jason, there's nobody on the other side of the mirror today. This is just me and you. I will only say this once. Aside from the RICO stuff, we really don't have anything on you. We tried, but we cannot actually tie you to anything criminal. We don't know how you personally make your money, but it does not seem to come from the drugs. Now we could still try you on the RICO stuff, and we could probably convict you. Your so-called brothers are going to go down hard."

He paused, leaned forward and put his hands on the table. "With that being said, I know that if you had outed me to your club at the party that night, I would never have gotten out alive. You let me go when you didn't have to. In return, I'm going to let you go. This is your one chance to wake up and smell the coffee. Straighten yourself up. Get out of this life. You won't get this chance again." With that, Agent Tyler turned to leave the room.

"What happened to Rat?" Jason asked, his first words in two days.

Tyler stopped short of the door. He turned slowly back toward Jason and said, "He came out of his bedroom with an AK-47. He shot two agents, but neither was seriously hurt. He was killed on the scene."

Jason looked down at the floor as he mourned the wasted life of his brother. Agent Tyler slipped quietly from the room, leaving the biker to his thoughts.

EPILOGUE

On a warm June morning in Paris, Tennessee, Jason Broaduc, aka Forty-Five of the IRON KINGZ Motorcycle Club, fired up his 2004 Harley Davidson Road Glide. As the engine rumbled beneath the seat in Ape-Hangers' parking lot, he took one last look at the building. It was the site of his introduction into the outlaw world. Boarded up now, it looked cold and drab despite the bright morning sunlight. Gripping the throttle atop his handlebars, he pulled onto the highway and left in search of peace.

He and five other IRON KINGZ had survived the bust that took the club down in April, and they were all heading to a new city to regroup. Greenville, Mississippi was in the heart of the Delta. It would provide an out-of-the-way harbor for them while the spotlight was still shining brightly on their brothers awaiting trial. The cancer had taken Lex during his first week in jail. He and Rat were the only club members other than those on the road this morning that would not stand trial.

Jason felt the warm Tennessee air on his face as he raced down Highway 79, with the rest of the free IRON KINGZ behind him. It was good still being among brothers who truly had his back.

About the Author

Troy Mason is a retired United States Marine, Iraq War Veteran, and an avid biker, logging over 20,000 miles per year on his Harley-Davidson. He lives in Virginia. This is his first novel.

http://outlawauthor.com